THE MYSTERY OF
IRELAND'S EYE

A DYLAN MAPLES ADVENTURE

THE MYSTERY OF IRELAND'S EYE

SHANE PEACOCK

NIMBUS
PUBLISHING
— NIMBUS.CA —

Nimbus Publishing Limited
3660 Strawberry Hill St., Halifax, NS, B3K 5A9
(902) 455-4286 nimbus.ca

Printed and bound in Canada

NB1372
Cover design: Cyanotype Book Architects
Interior design: Heather Bryan

This story is a work of fiction. Names, characters, incidents, and places, including organizations and institutions, either are the product of the author's imagination or are used fictitiously.

Library and Archives Canada Cataloguing in Publication
    Peacock, Shane, author
    The mystery of Ireland's Eye / Shane Peacock.
    Originally published: Toronto: Viking, 1999.
    ISBN 978-1-77108-615-8 (softcover)

 I. Title.
PS8581.E234M97 2018   jC813'.54   C2018-901380-X

Nimbus Publishing acknowledges the financial support for its publishing activities from the Government of Canada, the Canada Council for the Arts, and from the Province of Nova Scotia. We are pleased to work in partnership with the Province of Nova Scotia to develop and promote our creative industries for the benefit of all Nova Scotians.

For Johanna,
conceived in a random act of love.

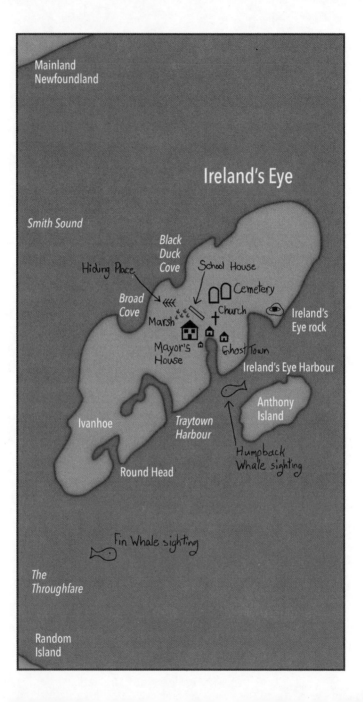

TABLE OF CONTENTS

1. In the Eye of the Storm 1

2. How It Began 8

3. An Ominous Warning 29

4. Monsters Beneath Us 42

5. A Frightening Feeling 61

6. The Magical Island 73

7. Ghosts 87

8. Terror in the Graveyard 112

9. A Night to Remember 119

10. Villains 128

11. The Chase 143

12. A Race Against Time 153

13. The Boy 166

1

IN THE EYE
OF THE STORM

When we pushed off from the shores of Random Island the water was calm and friendly. But now, with Ireland's Eye still a shadow on the horizon, the waves were growing higher by the minute. I clenched my jaw tightly and my hands shook as I dug in with the paddle: I was trying not to think of the dangers that lay ahead. Our kayaks were pointing straight out into the Atlantic.

My mother and father were on either side of me. She was glancing anxiously my way between strokes, searching for any signs of nervousness, and I could see him ploughing forward just off my nose, staring intently at the swells in the water, wondering if this was too much for me. I looked towards our distant destination, my heart pounding. No matter what happens and no matter what they say, I'm not giving up: what lies ahead means too much to me.

But in minutes the waves had grown even more, rising in front of us like foothills, their peaks nearly a metre high.

"Keep paddling," yelled Dad. "Keep yourself on top of the waves!"

I did as he said and suddenly I was going twice as fast as I had ever gone in a kayak, shooting along on top of the waves like a surfer. In any other circumstance this would have been exciting, but I knew that falling into the icy waters of the ocean might be fatal and that if I couldn't keep up with the waves, if I got between them, they would pitch me overboard. So I kept paddling, as hard as I could. But then the crosswinds started.

Up on top of a wave, gusts whipping across my bow, I felt the kayak move sideways. It made me feel out of control and that isn't something you ever want to feel on the ocean. Dad had warned me about it.

"If you ever feel a loss of control, Dylan," he said while we were practicing at home, "tell me and we will stop, wherever we are."

I had to fight to keep myself from shouting for help, from crying out that I would never make it: I was on the verge of absolute panic. The kayak was not only being shot forward by the growing waves but rocking sideways at the same time. Then another frightening thought began making its way into my mind: I was starting to think about how many metres of water were beneath me. Dozens? Hundreds? Thousands?! A weird kind of fear of heights washed over me, adding to my problems. It seemed as though I had just stepped off the top of a skyscraper, countless storeys in the air. There was nothing between me and the dark ocean floor but an ever-shifting mile of liquid. I glanced over at Mom. She was staring at me with a frightened expression on her face.

"Dylan! Are you okay?" came her yell through the wind and spray.

I couldn't say anything. I turned my face back towards Ireland's Eye and kept paddling like a zombie, surfing on waves that were over a metre high now, and still growing.

We were well off the coast of Canada, out in the Thoroughfare, a sometimes-treacherous stretch of water several kilometres across that lies between the friendly shores of big Random Island and the distant, barren little Eye. Back in another time fishermen and sailors had to navigate through here just to do their jobs, fighting their way around this end of Random to get from its sheltered north channel to its south, or vice versa. Almost no one came this way these days unless they were well equipped with big, motorized boats, safe and powerful. The Thoroughfare is exposed to the winds of the mighty Atlantic, and when you come out of the gentler waters of the channels, it can hit you like a sandstorm. We had known all along that it could be dangerous, but we hadn't counted on its deceptiveness. The Thoroughfare had fooled us and now it had us in its grip.

In front of us Dad was motioning towards a small island. It was off to his left and had a little cove. We made for it. In five minutes, as we came into the cove's protection, the waves had lessened a little. We pulled the kayaks together for a conference, bobbing around and banging into each other. Big drops of rain began plopping down on us, and then fell much harder, sounding like mini-machine-gun fire on the fibreglass.

"Are you all right, Dylan?" shouted Dad.

"Yes," I said, the colour coming back into my face.

"Do you want to go on?" asked Mom.

"Yes."

She looked at me for a long time. "I don't think so," she finally said to Dad. "This is too much for him. It's too much for me!"

"I'm afraid we don't have any choice now," shouted Dad. "It's farther back to Random Island than out to the Eye. We have to make a run for it!"

"But why don't we just try landing here?"

Dad glanced towards the shore. "We can't land anywhere here, not with these waves and that rocky shoreline. And if we stay in this cove the swells are soon going to be worse than the waves."

So we had no choice.

"How far away is Ireland's Eye?"

"About half an hour in this stuff."

And so we went forward, back out into the storm, fighting for our lives. Fifteen minutes later, I was worn out but paddling with every ounce of energy I had, riding waves nearly two metres high, when Ireland's Eye began to show itself. It seemed to come up suddenly in the rain and the wind, like a magical creature hiding itself until you could see the whites of its eyes. Crashing forward I noticed a caribou standing on the shoreline in the wind, staring out at us. There *is* life after all, I thought, on this mysterious island.

But it was doubtful now if we would ever get near it. The closer we got to our destination the more the storm seemed to rage, as if it were trying to keep us away from the Eye, warning us to leave it be.

A few minutes later, as we struggled along the southern shore, I noticed Dad out of the corner of my eye churning up beside me.

"Don't look at me!" he yelled. "Keep looking straight ahead! In five minutes, when we get near those rocks to your right, we are going to turn left and head towards the island! That's where the town was! That's where we can land! Mom's going in first, then you, and I'll bring up the rear!"

I didn't say anything this time either. My eyes were fixed on each wave as it rose up, and on the bow of my kayak as it lifted out of the water and then crashed down.

Mom darted in front of me and led the way. In a few minutes we began turning and then I could see the entrance to the island! But just as we approached the opening, the storm seemed to turn to gale force. The waves became mountains, so high I could no longer see anything, not Mom or Dad, or even Ireland's Eye. A force that felt like a hurricane picked me up and lifted me high into the air. I twisted sideways, my kayak almost above me, desperately out of control. Then I felt myself going down.

2

HOW IT BEGAN

It was nearly a year ago when my father first told me about Ireland's Eye. We were at our cottage on a hot and lazy summer day, motorboats buzzing by and Sea-Doos thump-thump-thumping over any wakes they could find, and Dad was sitting in a lawn chair on our deck, absorbed in another book. That's what he's like: he's either reading everything in sight, or he's off on some adventure, climbing a mountain or crossing a lake somewhere in the Yukon or Alaska or Timbuktu. And when he's not doing that, he's planning something. The book he was reading that day was about Newfoundland and I could tell he was getting an idea because he was tapping his foot, and then, and this is always the biggest giveaway, he started vibrating his whole leg. Suddenly he jumped up, ran into the cottage, and came out again, the screen door slamming behind him. My dad is old-fashioned about a lot of things. He was carrying a map in his hand and soon had it spread out on the deck, holding it in place by leaning over it on all fours like a kid. I saw his finger trace something and then stop decisively. He lowered his head closer to the map and smiled.

"That's it," he said excitedly.

I had been walking the other way on the deck, trying to decide whether I wanted to go for another swim or listen to some tunes on Mom or Dad's phone, but I couldn't miss this.

"What are you doing, Dad?" I asked.

"Nothing."

That's my pop, forty-five years old and going on ten.

"*What* are you *doing*?"

You have to get his attention.

"I'm looking at a map of Newfoundland."

I came up to him and peered over his shoulder. His finger was pressed so firmly onto the map that it was turning white at the tip. I squatted down to see what he was pointing at. He hardly noticed.

Newfoundland looked to me like the head of a moose, with a single thick antler going up at a cool angle, while down at his neck there were things hanging down, like whatever those things are on a rooster's neck. My father had his finger just above them and almost out in the Atlantic Ocean, at the eastern end of the land. At the tip of his finger I saw a little island and then a smaller one. I leaned even closer, my cheek resting against Dad's wrist. "Ireland's Eye," it read.

"What's that? What's Ireland's Eye?"

When my father is interested in something a jet airplane could fly a foot over the cottage and he wouldn't even notice, unless of course the vibrations disturbed whatever he was looking at. So I resorted to desperate measures. I moved the map.

"Hey!" he said. "What are you doing?"

"What's Ireland's Eye?" I asked again.

He stared at me blankly for a moment. "Did you just ask me that?"

I smiled at him.

"Sorry. Uh…it's an island in Trinity Bay in Newfoundland, almost out in the Atlantic."

"And you think it's cool, don't you, Dad?"

"It's very cool."

"Why?"

"Well, first of all because it's an island, and you know I like islands. And secondly because no one lives there. And thirdly…."

My father is a lawyer, but he wishes he wasn't. He loves dramatic things and he likes to be dramatic himself, at least at home. At work he is John A. Maples, respected barrister and solicitor, always very serious, and bored. As he told me about Ireland's Eye, he paused with all the drama he could muster, and then said:

"…because…right at its centre…way out there, on the edge of the Atlantic Ocean…*there's a ghost town!*"

And that was when I knew I had to go there.

I didn't know why. It didn't make any sense for a twelve-year-old to go out into the ocean in a kayak, not with the waves and swells I would have to face. And it seemed pretty well impossible that my parents would let me go, especially Mom: she would freak out if I even brought up the idea. She'd go herself, of course. If Dad was going, she'd be there.

But something was telling me I had to see Ireland's Eye too, not a voice or anything like that, just a feeling, something that made goosebumps come out on my skin and made me feel funny in my stomach when Dad said, "…way out there, on the edge of the Atlantic Ocean…

there's a ghost town!" I knew there was something on that island I just had to see.

"You're going, aren't you, Dad?"

"You bet, Dylan. By this time next year, we'll be turning that corner out of the windswept waves of the Atlantic and looking up at the serene beauty of Ireland's Eye, a vision of what has been in the distance."

My father can get poetic when he's in the mood. "Next year, eh?"

But he was lost in the map again, seeing himself battling the ocean, feeling the first sighting of the ghost town on the hill.

Next August I would be thirteen years old. I had a whole year of growing, of maturing, of learning to be a good kayaker and an excellent swimmer. But most importantly I had a year to convince them that I should go too. As for Ireland's Eye, whatever it was that drew me grew stronger with every day.

BOTH DAD AND I needed something to distract us that year. My grandfather had died in the spring and we both missed him terribly. Grandpa had been just about my best friend. Saturday nights in the winter we often got together at his house to watch hockey. We rarely missed a game. Grandma had never been a hockey fan, Mom thought it was too violent (I don't know what she based that on, since I don't think she ever saw a single game), and Dad felt that watching anything was a waste of time. "Why watch what you can do?" he used to say, though he never played the game.

So Grandpa and I were a little island of excitement on hockey nights at his house, with a calm, rational, slightly disapproving sea of sensible relatives all around us. We loved the colour, the speed, the courage, and the inventiveness of what we watched, and for those few hours we were like one person, and I think that person was very young.

The only thing we disagreed about was the history of the game. I wasn't very impressed by stories about old players who would never play again. I loved what was happening *now*, what was speeding around in front of me on the TV. That was it. Grandpa knew this and tolerated it, and he tried to find ways to make me listen to his stories. A Gordie Howe story, for example, would start with, "You know, Sidney Crosby is pretty good, only Howe was better. I recall the time…" and off he would go, while I shut my ears and watched Crosby rocket-power down the ice, leave a defenceman in his vapour trail, fire a laser into the top corner, and pump his fist in the air as a funky bass line throbbed through the arena.

Grandpa was born in the 1930s, but it was the '40s and early '50s he loved to talk about. That was when the Leafs were the undisputed kings. Six Stanley Cups in ten years, led by a gentleman without peer named Syl Apps, the heroic young "Billy the Kid" Barilko, frozen in time and immortal at the tender age of twenty-four, and of course, Grandpa's favourite, Teeder Kennedy. Hard-driving, never-say-die number nine, the glorious captain. The spirit of Teeder Kennedy, in Grandpa's eyes, was still alive and well.

I heard all of this and much more, time after time. I nodded my head as we watched TV, and his stories went in one ear and quickly out the other.

"The history of the game," Grandpa would say, "has to be valued. History should be valued throughout life. The people who came before us made important contributions."

"Sure, sure," I said to myself, stifling a yawn, "but they're dead."

And now…so was he.

I missed him at my own games. We were both centres and we used to talk about why it was the best position. You had so much more freedom. And you had to be a good skater, none of this up and down the wing, or stay at home and mind your own zone. Wingers and defencemen had to put up with that, but *we* were free to use our imaginations on the ice. A centreman can almost feel the wind in his face, even in a stuffy arena. We can skate anywhere: up and down, behind the net, in front of it, crisscrossing back and forth, moving the play in one direction or turning it around and sending it the other way. The game always has a flow to it, whether it be fast, slow, or jerky, and centres can join it, work in it or against it, even slip in and out of it. Grandpa used to say that a centreman was the artist on the team, but a tough artist, of course.

I had a pretty good season, despite missing him. And I know what it was that made me play well. It was Ireland's Eye. I'd look for Grandpa at the spot in the rink over the penalty box where he used to stand, a cup of coffee in his hand, never shouting, just watching me closely. For an instant I'd be shocked not to see him. Then I'd remember he was gone, so I'd think of Ireland's Eye.

To get there I would have to have the strength, skills, and maturity of an adult, and it would have to show. So even on the ice I worked at being more grown up: I took fewer penalties, I was more of a team player, I took power skating lessons, and spent hours practicing my wrist shot. Gone were the temper tantrums, the big celebrations after a goal, and all the board-banging slapshots. Dad didn't know much about hockey, but I convinced him to come to a few games, and on the way to the rink I'd talk about how the more mature players performed. Then I tried to show him that I was that sort of player. I doubted at first that he noticed. I'd look over at him and he'd have his usual dreamy look on his face, his mind off in the clouds thinking up another adventure. But one day on the way home he surprised me.

"Dylan, I see what you mean."

He is given to that sort of comment: just blurting out something that doesn't seem to be related to anything that anyone has said for the last year or so. I gave him my blank look, the one I use when he says that kind of thing.

"Oh, explanation, right? I mean that I see what you're saying about playing hockey in a mature way. You're doing it. Keep up the good work."

And that was all he said. But I soared. I doubt he knows how I soared. I could have lifted right out through the closed sunroof of the spotless Jeep he drives.

That's the first step, I thought to myself. *I'm on my way to Ireland's Eye.*

THE FOLLOWING WEEK I made my next move. This time I worked on Mom. It seemed to me that that was a good strategy. Once I'd sprung the question on them, I didn't want one of them trying to convince the other that I should go. No, I wanted both parental units on side at the same time and well aware that I was prepared for the trip.

A lot of Dad's adventures are on water, but Mom's the best swimmer. She was excellent in high school and university and just missed going to the Olympics by a hundredth of a second or something like that. She was the one who taught me to swim, and she used all sorts of ways to get me to have proper technique and even tried some motivational things on me. I can remember her talking for hours about an "approach" called "visualization." But I just wanted to swim and have fun, so right from the beginning I only messed around in the water. I had her genes, I guess, and it came to me easily, but I never took it too seriously and I suppose I could have been much better.

"Mom," I said to her one day when she had a moment, "I'd like to take swimming lessons."

Well, the look on her face should have been captured by a camera. She had this stunned expression and seemed to stare right through me as if someone on the other side of my head had spoken to her using my face.

"I thought I just heard you say you'd like to take swimming lessons," she said and laughed. "I'm sorry, what did you really say?" My mom is like that. She's a bit of a card, though a lot of the things she says that are funny are usually a little critical too: sarcastic, as they call it. I think it's because she's trying to keep Dad and me in line. We're both dreamers, I guess, and she has to put our feet on the ground from time to time. I think it's also her way of getting close to me. She's not a touchy-feely sort of mom, thank god, at least not constantly. Every now and then she gets into a bit of cuddling, but for the most part she just tries to kid me and pokes me in the ribs and that sort of thing. It's like she's telling me I'm not a little boy anymore, as if I'm on my way to becoming a man. But there are still some days, when she's particularly busy with her work, that I catch her looking over at me a lot with sappy looks, like she'd like to spend the whole day hugging me. She doesn't seem like a kidder then. On those days I try to keep my eye on her, in case of a surprise attack.

But I didn't need to worry today. She was in full joker mode.

"That's what I said," I told her in the most serious voice I could muster. "I'd like to take swimming lessons."

"Excuse me, but have you seen my son Dylan around?"

Good old Mom.

"Mom, I'm serious." Another very mature voice, matched with my most adult look.

My mother is always in a rush. She runs a private school downtown for parents who want their children to get what she calls an "alternative education." Don't ask me what that is. But it keeps her pretty busy. It isn't often that she or Dad actually sit and talk with me, except at dinner, of course. But this time I had Mom down for the count. I had Laura S. Maples exactly where I wanted her.

"Have a seat, Mr. Serious," she said. She looked at me for about a minute straight. I tried another grave expression.

"What do you want?" she finally said.

"Mo-om!"

"Okay, okay." Another pause. "Swimming lessons, Dylan? Are you sure?"

"I want to better myself, Mom."

She almost laughed. That wasn't a good sign. And yet I had the feeling we were moving in the right direction.

BY THE END OF January my hockey team was in first place, I'd been named team captain and I was, much to my mother's shock, the best swimmer in my swimming class. It was time for my next move.

In a way this move had started in September, but I knew Mom and Dad hadn't really noticed. They aren't bad parents as parental units go and if I have any problems they're always there to help. They often tell me how much they love me (I could do with a little less of that in public places), they hardly ever raise their voices at me, and they talk a lot about "giving me space" and "respecting me," and they do. But sometimes I wish they'd just haul off and yell at me. All their nice comments, which they make even when they're gritting their teeth because I'm really bugging them, can start to sound like they're taken from a book or something. I'd prefer it if they'd really notice what I'm doing, and then look me straight in the eye and tell me if it sucked. Anyway, this is a roundabout way of saying that they hadn't clued in to how much better I'd been doing at school lately and how much more time I'd been spending on homework. As usual, I had to spring it on them. For my target, I picked Mom again. She gave me the perfect opportunity.

Her car was running in the driveway when I got home that day and as I came through the front door she was banging around in the upper hallway, trying to get on the latest shoes her chiropractor had given her. I waited at the bottom of the stairs, smiling, my plan in place. Down the stairs she came, ready to fly out the door.

"Hi, sweetheart," she said, breathless. "Love you." That meant she was about to kiss me, hug me, and disappear. But I knew better.

"You need to see this," I said, using another very serious, mature expression. (I was getting better at those.)

She really did have to go. A board meeting or something like that. But when she saw the report card and heard my tone of voice, she knew she had to spend a moment with me. I could feel her frustration, but she smiled at me and did a wonderful job of hiding it. My mom would hang out with me all the time if her schedule let her, but she can't and that really upsets her. She plucked the card away from me, glanced at it and handed it back. Then she snatched it away again.

"This," she snapped, "is a forgery!"

I didn't take the bait. Instead I just waited, silent. That was the first time I'd ever seen my mother a bit flustered in my presence. She looked at me in a strange way.

"Let me know when you see Dylan around. I'd like to talk to him."

But it was an old joke and she knew it. So she gave up. Putting her hands on my shoulders she spoke in a voice she had never used with me before. It was the adult-to-adult tone I often heard when she was talking business on the telephone.

"You are growing up, Dylan," she said. "You are maturing right in front of my eyes."

Bingo.

Later, lying in bed in the darkness, strengthening my wrists by squeezing two parts of a rubber ball I had cut in half, I heard my parents talking in the kitchen. I slipped out of bed, pulled the door open a crack, and listened. They were discussing the improvement in my marks and how I seemed to be so different lately. My plan was working perfectly.

But I still had more to do. For the next phase I went after Dad again.

EVERY SPRING DAD RENTED a small indoor public pool in a little town just north of the city and practiced kayaking. He always went late at night just after public swimming had ended. Mom didn't go with him very often. She wasn't a kayaking fanatic and felt that the practice she had every summer at the cottage was enough. But occasionally Dad would ask me to come along, on the days when he knew the lifeguard had to be in the office and didn't have a direct view of the pool. I was to be the alarm bell should any emergency happen during one of his fancy manoeuvres, such as the rolls he loved to work on. So I trudged along with him, sullen and resentful about losing a night to such dreary duty, content to lie on the floor at one end of the pool listening to music on my earbuds or reading a comic book. He'd splash around like a kid, throwing water up over the edge, taking everything so seriously you'd swear he was doing this for some sort of world championship.

I didn't wait for him to ask me that spring.

"Dad," I said to him one day in late February, a good six weeks before he usually rented the pool, "when are we going kayaking?"

Well, that got his attention, let me tell you. Though his head was buried in some mountain-climbing magazine that would normally arrest his attention the way a loaded gun pointed between the eyeballs would focus anyone else's, he turned to me immediately. His head snapped around as though I'd just mentioned that

I was a *Tyrannosaurus rex*. It wasn't just that I'd asked about kayaking practice and asked so cheerfully, it was the fact that I'd said "we."

"Huh?" he said, looking very stunned.

I smiled as pleasant a smile as I had in my repertoire. "When are we going kayaking, Dad?"

"Kayaking? You and me? Kayaking?"

"I can hardly wait."

"You can hardly wait?" he repeated in a monotone, that stunned look not entirely gone from his face.

"Let's start earlier this year, Dad."

And so we went together just a few weeks later, my dad so amazed that I don't think he really believed I would show up for our first practice. But when the day arrived so did I, right on time, waiting in the Jeep as he climbed in shaking his head. Every week for the rest of that spring the two of us splashed around in that pool like a pair of children, threatening to flood the whole building.

By the time we were ready to go to the cottage that summer my stroke was stronger, I felt at home in the kayak and I could roll it nearly as well as Dad. Occasionally, while he was working on something, I'd swim a few laps in the pool, going as hard as I could, making as much noise as I could, churning up the water like a speedboat. I could feel him watching me, his mouth wide open.

MY FRIENDS THOUGHT I was nuts too. I didn't really have time to do the things I used to do anymore. Things like killing time playing video games. That really ticked off Rhett and the Bomb. That's Rhett Norton and Bomb Connors, my two best buds, a slightly thick defenceman and a right winger with a big boomer of a slapshot. They used to love the nights when Dad was off kayaking at the pool on his own and Mom was at a meeting. We had the TV, the fridge, and anything else we wanted in the house all to ourselves. We were in heaven.

But I guess it almost seemed to them like I had changed overnight. Before long they were bugging me about all the homework I was doing and why I was doing it, and when they got really peeved they even called me a suck about my marks. But I knew they were impressed that I was team captain now, and I'm sure that once or twice when I called I actually caught them working late at night on their own school work, though they denied it every time.

"What's with you and this Ireland's Eye thing anyway?" asked Rhett one day as he and the Bomb stood at my door with their boards, unable to coax me out for a little skate down to the mall. I'd told them and only them (you can never be too careful) about my Ireland's Eye project almost the day after Dad showed me the map, and every day since then. I guess they were getting pretty sick of it. (To be honest, I also told my other best bud, Jason Li, left winger, good moves… and Terry Singh too, but goalies are good at keeping secrets.)

"Yeah," said Bomb. "All it is is a little island somewhere in Newfie land. We can't waste this whole summer. We're going to be grade eights next year, man, we've got to have some serious fun before school. You can't go back in September and say you spent all your time in Nowheresville. Look at all the things we could do if you didn't go."

"Remember last year, when John A. and Laura S. were out west climbing that friggin' mountain?" said Rhett. "Your grandparents were pretty cool about letting you do things. And we're a year older now."

"Grandpa's dead, okay?" I snapped, never pleased when that subject came up.

"Then stay with your grandmother, Maples, she's a pushover!"

"I'm going to Ireland's Eye," I said firmly.

They just didn't understand. I suppose in a way I

didn't either, so it was hard to blame them. But somehow I knew that exploring that strange island was going to be so much better than playing video games all summer, or skateboarding until we dropped, or even going to a few Blue Jays games. It was just something I had to do. Rhett and the Bomb and Jason and Terry would still be at home when I got back. They'd forgive me and we could do the same things we'd done before. But Ireland's Eye…*way out there, on the edge of the Atlantic Ocean, there's a ghost town*…it was like something from a dream.

So, I kept working on getting there.

ABOUT A MONTH INTO the cottage season, during which time I swam and kayaked every day, Mom and Dad gathered on the deck to plot the trip to Newfoundland.

I was in the water when I heard them say those two magical words. *Ireland's Eye.* I knew my moment had come. It was time to put it all together.

As I paddled quickly towards the shore their voices grew louder. They were talking about how difficult it would be to get from Random Island across the Thoroughfare to their little gem-like destination in the ocean. They sounded excited. Then they spoke of the Eye itself, and of the ghost town on the hill in the old harbour. I docked the kayak and got out.

My heart beat faster as I walked up the little incline towards them, carrying the kayak. They were seated at a table, their backs towards me, talking now about legends and rumours and history. I stepped up onto the deck and dropped the kayak loudly, almost knocking it into the table. They both looked up.

"I'm going with you," I said clearly, looking both of them in the eye.

Mom and Dad opened their mouths at the same instant, a "no" forming on their lips. But something stopped them. They looked at each other. It seemed to me that it was only then that they realized what I had been doing these last twelve months. And they knew my plan had worked.

I was going to Ireland's Eye.

3

AN OMINOUS WARNING

We had a wonderful trip to the east coast that August.
Even packing the Jeep seemed to go smoothly. No
one argued, nothing got lost, everyone was ridiculously
happy.

The place where we live in downtown Toronto is
called Moore Park. It isn't a bad stretch of real estate,
I must say, with lots of nice old brick and stone houses
(at least they're old to me), and tennis courts, lots of
trees, the Rosedale valley for walking your dog (having
fur and four legs and being able to bark and pee on a
fire hydrant made you pretty important in "the Park"),
that sort of thing, and lots of cool places for getting
your board airborne. Grandpa used to tease me that

Moore Park was okay, but didn't quite qualify me for being a rich guy. The poor would love to live there, he said, but wealthy folks would sneeze at it. I always thought that was kind of a funny expression, one from the old days, I suppose. My grandpa's parents didn't have much money and stuff when they were bringing him up and he never forgot it. He often said that when he was a kid he would have been pleased just to put up his tent in one of our backyards. Actually, we did that once, Grandpa and me.

Anyway, right from the moment we left Moore Park until we hit "the Rock" about a week later, we had amazing weather and everything went smoothly. I even had a decent time dealing with the parental units, locked up as I was with them in the Jeep. Of course, they made sure I had equal time in the front seat, and unfortunately told me how much they loved me every hundred kilometres or so, and resisted all impulses to yell at me even when I gave them some golden opportunities. They'd put a no-cellphone-rule into effect for the trip, so we all had to talk to each other. My mother was doing a lot more hugging than usual too—not just looking over at me anymore, she was going right at it. It was as if she had me at her mercy or something. But still, the week seemed to slip by.

Of course, a lot of that had to do with where my head was at, as Mom likes to say. Ireland's Eye seemed to be drawing me across Canada towards an unknown adventure that excited and terrified me at the same time. What was I going to find out there on that little island in the ocean? The lectures Dad gave as we passed each landmark (Mom soon started calling the trip the John A. Maples Lecture Tour), the scenery and even the people we met seemed like a blur, as though I was being pulled through a tunnel towards my destiny.

Maybe Dad's stories about the Eye, some of which were actually pretty good (especially the ones about the ghost town), were beginning to have an effect on me. The most bizarre thing he told me was about the citizens of Ireland's Eye and what happened to them. They were actually removed from their homes; not exactly forced to go, but sort of. It was a kind of political thing. What would Moore Park be like if that happened to us, if we all just left one day and many years later a bunch of people came to look around? What would they do when they got to our house? It would be broken down, I suppose, and full of cobwebs and really quiet. I wondered if they'd look in my room. Some of my stuff might still be there....That seemed like a pretty weird thing to be thinking about. It gave me the creeps.

At night on our trip I always dreamt of Grandpa. He appeared in Montreal, another time in Moncton, twice in Antigonish, and even when I slept for a few moments at North Sydney in Cape Breton waiting for the ferry to take us, our Jeep, and three kayaks out to the fabled Rock. Each time he begged me not to forget him, and I woke in a cold sweat, missing him desperately.

Newfoundland is called the Rock for good reason. Parts of it look a little like the moon, though I must admit I've never actually been on the moon. But the people are incredibly friendly, so friendly the three of us found them a little strange. We met dozens of Newfoundlanders on the boat and one man even invited us home for seal flipper pie and, believe it or not, cod tongues. We passed on that.

"My sunny b'y, this is some fine weather," said a man to me as we were tightening the boats on the roof of the Jeep after we docked at Argentia. I hadn't even looked at him and he just started talking to me. The accent was so thick I'd completely missed the first part of what he'd said.

"Yeah, it's okay," I replied, wondering if I should be talking to him. I noticed another man, a friend of his, standing nearby watching us. He was older, unshaven and silent.

"Lard tunderin', b'y, is that all you can say?" said the first man. "This is darlin' weather. The gods must be lookin' down upon Newfoundlanders this week, that's all I can say."

Of course that wasn't all he could say. He said enough in the fifteen minutes we worked on the roof rack to last a lifetime. He propped up one of his big muddy boots on the end of our Jeep and started firing out questions. The mud began gathering on Dad's polished bumper.

"You're from away, aren't ya?"

"No, sir, we're from Toronto."

"That's what I mean, darlin', you aren't from the island, are ya?"

"No, we aren't."

"Where are you headed with those little plastic dinghies?"

"Actually, they're kayaks, and we're going to Ireland's Eye."

Suddenly he went silent. His eyes narrowed and he looked right into me.

"Ireland's Eye?"

"Yes, sir."

"Why would you want to go there?" he asked, the friendliness completely gone from his voice.

Mom noticed the tension between us. She smiled as she tried to break it. "We hear it's a beautiful place," she said. But the man kept looking at me, saying nothing.

Dad came down from the side of the Jeep, walked up to us and gently pulled me aside. "We're going to see the ghost town," he said in a matter-of-fact voice.

"It's *my* policy," said a stern voice from behind the man, "to let ghosts be."

It was the older, unshaven Newfoundlander. His accent wasn't nearly as thick and he spoke each word slowly and carefully. He stepped forward, right between me and the other man. His white hair grew long and wild under his rain cap and he looked coldly at me with watery eyes. After a dramatic pause, he leaned his weather-beaten face down towards mine and brought his lips up to my ear.

"Do not go to Ireland's Eye," he said in a whispering, trembling voice. He lifted his head again, still staring at me. Then he motioned to the first man and they turned and walked away.

"What did he say?" asked Dad.

"Uh…he said…" I noticed I was shivering. "He said…to watch out for whales."

"Whales?" said Dad, laughing, obviously relieved. "I've dealt with whales before, Dylan. He just thinks we're greenhorns." He shook his head and laughed again. "Whales! Let's get going, gang."

But all the way up the Trans-Canada Highway I could hear that voice saying, *"Do not go to Ireland's Eye."* Now there was something pulling me away from my destiny with the same power as I was pulled towards it.

The weather was indeed wonderful. Every place we stopped people talked about it. They seemed to think that something strange was in the air.

"Life is always changing, my son," said a man in a St. John's Maple Leafs sweater who pumped gas at our first stop. "And that's why the weather is so changeable too—it's meant to be that way. You could say that here on the island our weather's *very* human: it changes by the hour. I tell you, there's something quare going on when she's sunny skies like these, days after days."

Newfoundland appeared to be in bloom, twenty-four hours a day. The sky was clear and the sun was out and the scenery, as we drove into hilly country, was breathtaking. Even the rocks seemed to disappear. There was bright blue sky and deep green trees and the blue ocean down below, crashing against the shore in great sprays of white.

We drove past places with names like Tickle Harbour, Come by Chance, and Goobies. But I wasn't amused by anything. Ireland's Eye isn't a funny name, I said to myself, not funny at all.

At Clarenville we stopped in at a store to get directions to a house in nearby Shoal Harbour. An old university friend of Dad's had arranged with a colleague of his to let us leave our Jeep in his garage while we were gone in the kayaks. Dad's friend had moved out to start a veterinary practice just north of St. John's about twenty years ago. He was married to a doctor and was raising three children on the Rock. He was also a fanatical kayaker. Several times he had made the dangerous trip around Random Island, the jumping-off point to Ireland's Eye. But for some reason he had never tried to get to the Eye, though it was just a few kilometres away.

"Why has Dr. Peacock never made it to Ireland's Eye?" I asked Dad as we pulled into the driveway.

"Oh, I don't know, maybe he's afraid of ghosts."

"That's not funny, Dad!" I blurted out. But he was gone, slamming the car door and running up the front walkway.

Mom turned to me. "Dylan, are you afraid? You don't have to do this, you know. We could make other arrangements for you and—"

But I cut her off. "I'm not afraid, Mom."

"Are you sure?" She looked into my eyes.

"I'm sure."

But I wasn't. I sat there silently as we drove the short distance to the launching point, near a causeway that went over to Random Island. Dad seemed really excited now, twisting his head down to look out the side window for glimpses of the water and nearly driving off the road a couple of times. But Mom kept turning around and looking at me. "Are you okay?" her eyes seemed to be saying. I tried not to look back. I wasn't going to blow this now.

We dumped the kayaks and all our food and supplies on the ground, and Dad took the Jeep back to the storage place in Shoal Harbour. While he was gone we started packing the boats, Mom watching me closely, the silence deafening. Dad returned, and when Mom figured I was out of range, she went over to him and whispered something. Then I could feel them eyeing me together. In a few minutes Dad came up to me.

"Hey, buddy, feeling all right?"

"Sure," I said.

"One hundred percent sure?"

"Yeah."

"Thought so," said Dad, smiling at Mom as if he'd won a bet or something. He went back to preparing the boats, whistling.

"Why don't we just kayak around here?" Mom said suddenly, dropping her paddle to the ground and looking at me.

"What?" Dad barked.

"What?" I said, trying to sound as upset as Dad.

"We really don't have to go to Ireland's Eye, John," Mom told Dad. "I feel guilty enough already." She glanced out towards the distant ocean horizon. "God knows what it's going to be like out there."

"Here we go with the guilt again," sighed Dad.

Guilty is a word my mom uses a lot. Often about me. She says she feels guilty about working so much, guilty about not seeing me enough. Sometimes you'd swear she was a criminal.

She pulled Dad aside and they started talking in a heated whisper this time. I could hear bits and pieces of it. Mom was saying that the only reason she agreed to let me come on the trip was that she felt the family needed to be together this summer, that work kept us all apart too much, and she wanted to be with her son every day for a couple of weeks straight. But now she was worried that that was a selfish decision and this trip was too much for me. She kept repeating in an anxious voice that they may have gotten me in over my head. Dad thought she was being kind of paranoid.

He maintained that I was a capable kid now and we should at least head out and see what happens—if things got bad we could turn around.

To be honest, though I was cheering for Dad, a tiny little part of me was hoping for Mom. What if I really can't handle this? That old man on the wharf at Argentia, he sounded like he knew the Eye, knew enough to stay away from it. *Do not go to Ireland's Eye.* Why did he say that to me? What in the world was out there?

But I couldn't come all this way just to give up now. Rhett and the Bomb would think I was a real horse's butt for starters. Get a grip, I told myself. I brushed my doubts aside and strode towards Mom and Dad.

"Excuse me!" I almost shouted at them.

"Yes?"

"Yes, dear?"

"You let me go on this trip because I proved I could go, right?"

"Right," said Dad firmly.

"Because I showed I could act responsibly and that sort of stuff, like a more grown-up person, right?"

"Right."

"Then quit whispering and talk to me."

There was a pause.

"Good point," said Mom. "It's just that you seem a little frightened."

"I'm not frightened, okay?"

"See?" said Dad.

"John, let me finish," sighed Mom, closing her eyes as she spoke to him. She opened them, turned to me and continued. "Listen, this may not be what you expect it to be; it isn't all adventure and excitement and the good guys winning, like a video game, you know."

"I know. Video games aren't like that anyway, Mom."

"I just mean this could be dangerous. Really dangerous. And if it is, we're turning around. Okay?"

I didn't say anything.

"Okay?" repeated Mom.

"Who decides if it's dangerous?"

"I do," said Mom and Dad together. Then Mom gave Dad a look. He made a motion like he was zipping his lips. "I do," she said quietly to me, without Dad chiming in. "Your father can paddle around the world if he wants and wrestle whales, but you and I are turning back if things get too bad. I don't want you, or me, to get so frightened we do something wrong. You are thirteen years old, you have your whole life in front of you." She paused. "Your dad's much older—he's at least fourteen." With that Dad grabbed Mom and started tickling her. "See what I mean!" she shrieked. She shoved him away, but then grabbed him and kissed him on the lips so hard it sounded like a cork coming out of a bottle. He stepped back, jammed his ball cap down on his head at a goofy angle and gave me a dumb smile. John A. Maples, respected lawyer.

I laughed. The tension seemed to be breaking.

"You've accomplished a great deal already, Dylan," said Mom, still glancing towards Dad as if he might try another tickle attack. Then she smiled at me. "You've proven yourself, you've met some big challenges. Whatever else we do is just icing on the cake."

The only icing on the cake I want, I told myself, *is putting my foot down in that ghost town in Ireland's Eye. I'll agree to this now, but if we get close and they try to make me turn back…I don't know what I'll do.*

"Okay," I said, putting on my best happy face, "let's get started."

"All right, Dylan!" shouted Dad. "Let's get your dry suit on!"

4

MONSTERS BENEATH US

Even on a hot summer day in August, with the water as smooth as glass, the Atlantic can kill a human being in a matter of minutes. The ocean doesn't really care how well you can swim, it will find another way to get you. Hypothermia, specifically. Mom and Dad had used and then explained that word to me many times over the past month; it described something we absolutely had to avoid. You get hypothermia when your body temperature drops so low that you freeze to death. Anyone who falls into the North Atlantic's frigid water has less than ten minutes to get back out. So dry suits are a must. They're made of rubber and are skin-tight, and they seal up your body completely, so that if you fall in you are not exposed to the water. While dry suits give you enough time to save yourself, they can't protect you forever: you must get out of the water as soon as possible. Mom and Dad and I had many times practiced what we would do if one of us was pitched out into the ocean. The person overboard hangs on to one of the other boats, while the two remaining kayakers pick up the capsized vessel, drain it, and then help the swimmer back into the cockpit. Everything must be done at top speed.

But there seemed little need for such desperate measures when we pushed off that day. We glided out from the launching spot near the causeway, did little semicircles on the eerily still water and headed under the bridge.

The northern shore of big Random Island was on our right, dotted with homes, while the mainland coast of Newfoundland was on our left, more than a kilometre away. We were moving east in Smith Sound, heading for the far end of Random, a part of the trip that would probably take us a few days. About halfway along, the population would start to dwindle and then completely disappear. Then we'd hit the Thoroughfare, the winds, and the Atlantic, and rocky little Ireland's Eye would appear in the distance. That's when we'd make a run for it.

Though here in the narrow Sound we seemed sheltered, Dad had made it clear many times that we shouldn't expect things to go smoothly at any location, because in Newfoundland bad weather can appear without warning.

I tried to keep that in mind, but bad weather just didn't seem like even a remote possibility that day. As we floated forward, the motorboats buzzing past, the birds hanging quietly in the blue sky, problems seemed far away. An hour ticked slowly by and I started to relax. Even Mom seemed content. Ireland's Eye was still three or four days in the distance, and who was that old Newfoundlander anyway? Probably just an ordinary fisherman. I had never believed in ghosts, why should I start now, just because some geezer was full of old wives' tales? I laughed to myself and put my back into the kayaking, skimming along past Mom and Dad, challenging them to a little race.

It had been late morning when we started, so by a little past noon we began searching for a place to stop for lunch. We were well out into the Sound by then and it was widening, the villages on the faraway mainland side appearing and disappearing, getting less frequent and harder to make out. We hugged the shore of Random Island for safety, and though we continued to see the odd collection of houses on flat spots there, much of the land was growing steeper as we travelled, and the trees (coniferous, I recalled from science class) that stuck up in the moss and rocks were tall and green, as thick as a rug in places. At a cove where we spotted a stream spouting out of the rugged cliff, we pulled in and made a difficult landing. Here there was about three metres of flat rock for us to rest on while we ate.

Mom was giving us a break in the food department during this trip. She got up early every day at home and made me a pretty involved lunch, heavy on the healthy stuff. Dad and I often ran into each other at the fridge in the middle of the night, searching for something a bit more substantial. (Sometimes he tried to tell me he was really just up for a pee and happened to notice the fridge on the way by.) But Mom promised to let us eat what we wanted on the Rock. So, though potato chips and chocolate bars were as scarce around our house as dinosaurs, Dad and I had loaded up on them for Newfoundland.

We ate our sandwiches, laughed as we stood below a cool spring of water with our mouths wide open, and then gloried in the demolition of the saltiest, greasiest three-hundred-gram bag of chips in Canada. But within an hour, true to the rigorous schedule I had prepared myself for, we were off again.

It wasn't long after that that I started seeing something in the water. I had pushed on ahead of Mom and Dad so I could pause for a moment to give my rapidly cramping hands a chance to rest while the parental units caught up. I leaned forward and while looking at my aching fingers caught a glimpse of something coming towards me from the depths. Way down below the surface I could see a mushroom-shaped bag of some sort, the weirdest bag I'd ever seen. You could see through it and it looked as though it had veins; it moved as if it were alive, but just barely. As I peered into the water, mesmerized by it, my kayak continued to float forward. Suddenly there were hundreds, no, thousands of these shimmering things, some right next to me, others a little lower and more even deeper; down as far as you could see they congregated, masses of them. I started feeling afraid.

"Jellyfish," said Dad, smiling as he skimmed towards me.

"Aren't they beautiful?" added Mom, pulling up along the other side. "Look, you can try to pick them up but they always get away." She reached in and tried to lift one out. It flopped over her paddle, looking solid and liquid at the same time, and fell back into the water.

I stared down at the jellyfish again. They were hanging there in the depths of the ocean, looking half-dead. What would it be like to dive in, I thought. Down, down, past millions of jellyfish. The light from above would grow dimmer, until it was total darkness. All you would see would be these glowing, pulsing jellies surrounding you. You'd be in their world, dark and spooky and suffocating. I kept staring at the water, looking as far into it as I could.

Way down in the depths, miles down it seemed, something was moving towards me. A chill went through my body in the heat of the day as it started to come into focus: a human head, severed from its body, was flying towards me from the depths of the Atlantic. I couldn't take my eyes from it. As it rose, I slowly began to see its features. It was the face of an old man, turned in my direction. Up from the depths he floated, his face and body dripping with jellyfish. Suddenly I realized who it was: it was the old Newfoundlander who had whispered into my ear! I cried out and jerked away from the surface of the water. The kayak rocked violently.

"Whoa!" said Dad, as he grabbed the hull and steadied it. "What's the problem here?"

"Down there, the old man from the landing!"

"Down there?" Dad asked, looking at me like I was nuts.

I gathered myself and peered tentatively over the edge of my kayak into the water. There was nothing there but a sea of beautiful, harmless jellyfish, floating quietly around us.

"I think you saw a red one."

"A red one?"

"The red ones can be kind of scary at first. They look like some sort of monster if you're not used to them."

"I think they're beautiful," said Mom as she skimmed by. She had no idea that I had been spooked by them. I glanced at Dad. Neither he nor I was about to tell her. "Look!" she cried. "There's one right by your kayak, Dylan."

And there it was, a red jellyfish, with a face.

BY LATE THAT AFTERNOON we had made such progress that we were nearly halfway around the northern shore of Random Island. We were moving at an amazing rate, actually approaching the end of population on either side of us. Snooks Harbour and Waterville were behind, Britannia and Burgoyne's Cove were nearing. We had already gone a long way past the spot we had picked out for our first night's stay, so we brought our kayaks together in a triangle in mid-channel, pulled out our plastic-wrapped maps, and searched for another place to pitch our tent. We decided on a tiny island about three kilometres ahead. The sun was getting low, but we thought we could make it with time to spare.

Half an hour later, sprinting towards our destination, the last villages vanishing behind us, we started hearing a strange sound. It was mechanical, like a large machine grinding something up and then hurling it over a cliff in a thundering cascade. At first it was a distant sound, but each time we heard it, it was louder, echoing across the water in the darkening surroundings of this uninhabited territory; I imagined an evil giant of some sort, doing some terrible deed. We kept pushing forward, anxious to get to the island before total darkness. We looked all around as we moved, searching for the source of this spooky sound.

Slowly it became clear that it was coming from the top of a steep embankment to our left, on the mainland side. But we couldn't make out what was happening under the darkening sky. For a while, it appeared the sound had stopped. Then suddenly it came again, erupting almost on top of us. We looked up and saw a rain of rocks hurtling towards the kayaks. I almost screamed.

"It's a slate quarry," said my father, so calmly that his voice startled me. I could have sworn he was as anxious as me. At the top of the cliff a dumptruck had come into view, unloading the rocks—it was obvious that many wouldn't even hit the water, let alone come within a hundred metres of our kayaks. In the distance behind the truck, the quarry hummed, grinding slate.

Still, as we moved towards our little island, which we could now see dimly ahead of us, that quarry seemed an eerie place. Imagine working there, I thought, likely with just a few others, late at night out here in the wilderness, where you could shout and your voice would vanish, echoing down the channel and out into the Atlantic Ocean.

By the time we reached the island the sound of the slate quarry had disappeared into the night. Again we had a shaky landing but managed to get out of our boats without falling in. The fingerless leather gloves on my hands were covered with salt from the water and when I stood I nearly buckled. I was looking forward to sleep.

But there was a great deal to do before that sort of comfort. We had to get all the provisions, many wrapped in waterproof coverings, out of the sealed hatches in the kayaks, find the tent, locate a good spot to erect it, get it up, and then start a fire and make supper. Roasted marshmallows had been promised for dessert.

An hour later we were sitting around the fire, our hamburgers and canned peas almost ready, looking out over the grey quiet of Random Island and the channel. You could barely make out the land from the water, and a mist seemed to hang over everything. It was so silent that it felt like Mom and Dad and I were the only people in the world.

"That's the ocean, that way," said Mom, motioning with a cooking fork.

"So that's where we're headed?"

"In that general direction, my son, but not quite all the way to England. The last time I flew to London it made my arms pretty tired, so you can imagine kayaking the whole way."

Mom seemed to have fully regained her sense of humour.

"Ireland's Eye is out there," said Dad quietly, as if it were some ghost lurking in the night. He may have put a little extra drama into it.

"It is? Where?"

"I'm not sure. Let me see…maybe that's it. See where Random Island turns…up there to the right? Well, look out into the ocean from that turn…. Something's out there."

I peered into the night, leaning over so far I nearly singed my jacket in the fire. There was something out there all right, a dark shadow way off in the distance. I strained my eyes and for an instant I thought I could see smoke drifting upward. But how could I detect anything like that from this far?

"I doubt we can see it from here," said Mom. "You two are fantasizing."

"You're probably right," agreed Dad.

But I disagreed. "I can. I can see Ireland's Eye. And there's smoke coming from it."

"Well, if there's smoke coming from it, my boy," said Mom, "then it's on fire and we'd better find ourselves another destination. There hasn't been any smoke coming from there for nearly forty years."

"Maybe it's a campfire."

"And maybe Mickey Mouse and his friends are there too, with Goofy and the whole gang," whispered Mom, pretending she was deadly serious. Then she poked me in the ribs.

"It could be a campfire," said Dad, "but I doubt it. Not too many people go out to the Eye anymore. There used to be drug smugglers dealing out there, because no one could catch them so far away from the mainland, but all the books say the police have pretty well cleaned that up. I hate to say it, Dylan, but you're probably just seeing things."

"Those are the smoke rings of your mind, sweetie," said Mom and plopped a burger onto my plate.

Maybe.

We stopped thinking about Ireland's Eye and discussed tomorrow's leg of the trip. We had made extremely good time due to the calm weather. Dad had calculated that we would get to the launching point from Random Island either late in our third day or early in the fourth. Now he was thinking, because the evening seemed so still, that with another perfect day we might get there by tomorrow night.

It was completely dark now, and beyond the warmth and glow of our fire we could see almost nothing. The light of the moon only allowed us to make out dim shorelines. If it wasn't for the sound of the waves gently hitting our little island in the quiet, we could have been anywhere, and anything could have been going on around us. A thousand ghosts and goblins could have been staring at us, a sea monster could be eyeing us from nearby. Even the few trees on the mainland a kilometre away weren't being rustled by wind.

But out of the darkness a sound suddenly broke the silence. It was unlike anything I had ever heard before and it came from somewhere out in the channel. Dad stood up, knocking the last bit of his burger into the fire.

"What is it?" I shouted, my voice sounding so loud and so petrified in the silence that I was scared twice: once by the sound and again by myself. It was a hissing sound, like something of gigantic size breathing out in a threatening way. And then there was a crash as it splashed into the water. It sounded huge.

"Quiet!" said Dad. We all waited in the silence. Then that sound came again. *Phoosh!* And then the crash.

"It's a minke," said Dad dramatically.

"A minke! What the *hell* is a minke!"

"Dylan!" said Mom. "What the *hell* kind of language is that?"

Oh god, a minke! Mink-ee. It sounded like some sort of villain from *Star Trek* or something. A minke was coming after us in the night, just the three of us all alone in the wilderness where no one would even hear us scream!

"A minke is a whale," explained Mom in a monotone. She wasn't looking at me, almost as if she was afraid that I had turned into a lunatic. "Uh...we told you about minkes before we left." She sounded concerned.

They had, too. But I was getting so spooked I was forgetting things. A minke is a small dark-skinned whale with a bit of white on it, and can be up to nine metres long when fully grown. They are common in

Newfoundland, especially in channels like the one we were in. You are more likely to see them than humpbacks and fin whales, which are much bigger. Humpbacks make an enormous noise when they appear and sometimes lift the whole front of their bodies out of the water; they're about the size of a house trailer. Fins are even bigger trailers. We were obviously getting into whale territory and I wished I had seen this one, but there would be more, probably as early as tomorrow. I could hardly wait, because even that minke had sounded like some sort of monster of the deep.

I must have fallen asleep within two minutes of my head hitting one of the inflatable pillows we had brought along. And then another dream came. This time my grandfather was standing on the wharf at North Sydney watching Mom and Dad and me leaving for Newfoundland. He was in a huge cheering crowd and everyone was waving except him. He was talking, and I could hear him clearly, though all around people were shouting and whistling and throwing confetti. I kept pointing him out to Mom and Dad but they only laughed at what I said, either because they couldn't hear me or because they knew Grandpa was dead.

"Remember me, Dylan," said Grandpa, with tears in his eyes. "Remember me."

The dream was so awful that I was glad when I woke up. Mom and Dad were snoring away next to me and outside everything was quiet, so quiet it almost hurt my ears. Every time I went to sleep the dream came back.

The next morning we were up early, having bacon and eggs and granola for breakfast. It was another calm sunny day, so we packed up and shoved off as soon as we could, pointing our kayaks towards the horizon where Ireland's Eye loomed.

It couldn't have been more than five minutes before the first whale came. *Phoosh! Crash!*

"THERE SHE BLOWS!" yelled Dad, as excited as a kid. When I darted my head around I saw his paddle pointing towards the Random side, but no whale.

"I didn't see it!"

"Just wait. They often come up again about a hundred metres farther on. This one was behind us so he should show up nearly even with the boats. His path is over here on this side, about fifty metres away. He's a minke, but he's a big one!"

My heart raced and I glued my eyes to the spot where Dad was pointing.

"About...NOW!" said Dad the whale expert. There was a long silence. We all stopped paddling.

PHOOSH.

"WOW!" I shouted. I couldn't help myself. I had never seen anything like it. A fish one hundred times normal size broke from the water where there had only been calm, rolling up from the depths and shooting air from its blowhole. It looked like a monster.

It went down again with a crash.

I'd seen a lot of movies but never a special effect quite like this.

"That's a whole lot of fish!" cried Dad.

"Mammal," said Mom the teacher dryly.

"Wow!" I said again.

BUT THAT WAS JUST the start of the whales. They seemed to come in crowds after that, though all of them were minkes. We kept making good time, moving quickly towards our destination as if pushed by something. And these whales were the best in-flight film you could order. But after a while Mom started losing her enthusiasm for them, especially because Dad would furiously paddle off after them whenever they surfaced, trying to get as close as possible. I wanted to follow. The first time I tried, Mom stopped me.

"Dylan!" she shouted. "Stay with me. If your father wants to kill himself that's up to him."

"Kill himself?"

"Whales have no interest in hurting people, but they can do you in without even noticing you are there. They have a sonar they use to find out how deep the water is and how far it is to each shore. But these guys have been in these coves and channels so often they actually shut their sonar off. They've got it all scoped out. And motorboats and big ocean liners don't bother them because those boats are so loud and so large that the whales sense them long before they see them. But kayaks? What do you think they sense when they're near a kayak?"

"I don't know."

"Nothing."

"Nothing?"

"They could come up from about a hundred metres below and hit you without even knowing you were there. They could break your kayak in half, and maybe you with it."

Now even these wonderful whales were scary.

"I want you to do something for me—" But before she could finish a minke surfaced, less than the length of a football field in front of me.

"Bang your paddle on the kayak!" Mom shouted.

I looked at her and didn't move.

"BANG YOUR PADDLE!"

Mom doesn't often roar like that, so I started banging. "Now start heading towards the shore. That one's coming RIGHT at you!"

Seconds after those words left her mouth the minke appeared again, up from the depths like a huge torpedo…three metres to the right of my boat! It was probably the scariest moment of my life, to that point. And my mom actually screamed.

I'd never heard her do that before.

So here I was, my mother letting go a bloodcurdling shriek, a whale three metres to starboard, and me frozen like a fish stick. But mixed in with the terror I felt was a sense of awe. I couldn't believe the size of the minke. He was like a couple of Zambonis. He came up nonchalantly, seemed to look at me with an eyeball not much bigger than my own, blew off his steam, and then began his disappearance, a rolling sort of exit where he shows you his back before he dives. And just like that, in a second or two, he was gone, back to his world in the depths. The kayak barely rocked, as if the minke had said, "Oh, hello there. Sorry…I'll make this smooth for you." I sat there transfixed by what I had seen. My mother was calling to me, but it seemed as if she were in another world, or like I was dreaming and she was awake. But then I heard my father, shouting as he sped towards me.

"DYLAN! Dylan, what was that like? Dylan, what did he look like up that close?"

"Perhaps we should see if he is alive first?" That was Mom coming from the other direction, glaring at my dad.

I turned and waited for the whale to come up again behind me. Soon I saw him break the surface, his body still faced in the same direction, his motion exactly the same as before, undisturbed by his confrontation with me. I don't know whether it was my imagination or not, but I thought he tried to look back a little, to see if I was still there. But then he was gone again.

Dad was whispering to me, "Tell me about it later." Then he raised his voice. "Your mother is right, Dylan. You have to be more careful."

"Oh, give it a rest," said Mom. "Let's move on."

But I let them get far ahead for a while. I kept looking back, watching my whale breaking the surface with a perfect pace, until he looked tiny in the distance.

5

A FRIGHTENING FEELING

The weather continued to be eerily beautiful. And soon the whales decreased in number and then stopped appearing altogether. Our picnics out there long past population were wonderful. We were surrounded by a warm and friendly nature. We even took off our dry suits, put on some suntan lotion, and stuck our life jackets under the elastic strings on the tops of the kayaks. Back in the water, we moved forward at a pace that seemed almost unbelievable, as if we were being pulled towards the island by a magnet. Dad was thrilled and Mom didn't seem to be worrying as much. But despite our progress, the Eye itself remained mysterious on the horizon, like a sort of little shadow that never got any closer or farther away. At times, when blocked by the curves of Random Island, it even disappeared. When we finally came to the corner, I somehow expected the Eye to show itself in all its glory, appearing before us with a flourish of magnificent music like in a movie. But it stayed small and distant, and partially obscured by little islands offshore.

Turning that corner was something we had dreaded. Out there you are actually beginning to come to the ocean. You leave the shelter of the Sound, enter the Thoroughfare, and see endless water in several directions. If you are headed east, your next destination could be Ireland, England, Spain, or Africa, and you can only imagine what it would be like to go a day or two in that direction, into a no man's land from which you might never return.

But all was peaceful when we made the turn. We stuck close to Random's shore. None of us said anything, waiting, it seemed, for the waves to start building. But they never did and we floated forward, now acutely aware of the distance we had put between ourselves and the mainland. It was a different world: it smelled different and the air, salty and cooler, seemed like the freshest air I had ever felt. The water looked silver, glinting as it rippled in the slight breeze. There were sheer rock cliffs on our right, rising over a hundred metres high, with little patches of grass here and there and evergreen trees at the top, dark and spooky. It could have been any time in history. We could have been back in the days when Indigenous people ruled this land, or even before, for all we knew. There was no sign of civilization.

The Beothuk people used to be scattered all over Newfoundland, but after the Europeans came they dwindled in number until finally there was only one. Imagine being Shanawdithit, the last Beothuk, alive in St. John's in the late 1820s, sitting there sad and lonely beyond compare, looking out at the white man's busy and noisy world, remembering a quieter past. Imagine her parents or her grandparents in their red-painted bark canoes, coming around this corner with Ireland's Eye in the mist behind them. Perhaps they would be hunting, their harpoons out and ready for a kill.

"Look up there," said Mom in a quiet voice.

I started. Then I looked up to where her paddle pointed and saw nothing. Just the dark tops of the trees. She motioned for me to move closer to the shore with her. We eased over and then I saw it.

Up on the very tip of the tallest tree sat a bird the size of our basset hound. But it didn't appear nearly as friendly. In fact, it looked evil. It was dark and its big metallic-looking beak was hooked and ugly. The head darted back and forth and the yellow eyes were so large that I could see them even from this far away. We drifted into the shadows next to the shore and heard the waves hitting the rocks. Suddenly the bird left the tree. I almost gasped: its wingspan seemed to be a couple of metres wide! For a few seconds it swooped towards our kayaks, examining us, checking to see if we were edible. Visions of this pterodactyl plucking us out of the water with its gigantic claws passed through my mind. Then it pulled up and ascended, soaring to an incredible height.

"That's a baby one," said Mom.

It was a bald eagle, the first one I had ever seen. For some reason I had thought they were extinct, or at least close to it, and certainly not living anywhere in Canada. It looked prehistoric to me. The adults I saw soon afterwards, noble with their white heads, were actually not as scary. I never forgot that first young eagle. As I watched him soar I wondered if he could see Ireland's Eye, and if his parents and their parents had seen it over the centuries as it changed, as people came there and then died, and as they began sadly moving away from their beloved homes. I wondered if he watched over the ghost town and the spirits who still surely lived there.

Now I was scaring myself. Where did all that stuff come from?

WE HAD PLANNED TO stop each night by five or six o'clock, but we were making such good time that we pushed on into the early evening, trying to get to our jumping-off point to the Eye, near the eastern end of Random Island. To our surprise, we made it with ease. Just as the sun was becoming a strange orange glow near the surface of the water, we approached a point that jutted out into the channel and Dad pulled out his plastic-wrapped map and made an announcement.

"We stop just up here."

He motioned to a cove on the far side of the point. We floated forward and slowly a natural harbour came into view. For a few minutes it presented a startling scene. The land was so much lower here, and there were great stretches of long grass like little fields among the rocks. The sight of a wharf sitting nearby, not in perfect shape, but far from decrepit, was almost shocking. A wharf out here in the wilderness—it was almost unbelievable. And that wasn't all: soon we saw rough paths in the grassland even a broken-down building or two. It dawned on me that I must be seeing my first ghost town.

We glided silently towards the wharf, holding our paddles up. Mom was still a little worried about me, so she started explaining.

"This isn't really a full ghost town. Most of the buildings have been taken away. There are only a few left now and even those are almost levelled. And there's a shack that people share when they get out here kayaking or boating or fishing. You'll see some lobster traps, I'm certain."

Sure enough, it wasn't long before one came into view, sitting not far from the wharf. I dreaded seeing a lobster struggling for life inside, but it must have been the wrong season, because the trap was tied down away from the water and it was empty.

"This is the real spirit of Newfoundland, right here," said Dad. "You wouldn't see this back home, unfortunately. Anyone who wants to use that shack can use it. And look up there."

I looked up the slight slope along a path that went away from the wharf and saw an old bus, without tires and colourfully painted, sitting well-grounded in a patch of grass among the rocks. It made me laugh.

"It's a bus, Dad! How'd they get a bus out here?"

"Oh, they've got their ways. That's not really a problem for a Newfoundlander. They could put the CN Tower out here if they had to."

Now *that* I'd like to see.

We landed and started exploring. It was good to get onto my feet again though I felt shaky, as had been the case at every stop. Your legs feel all rubbery and you kind of grope around at first for the land beneath you. But soon I was running, chasing Dad up the path past the two broken-down houses, making our way towards the shack. Mom was headed to the bus, shouting something to Dad about it reminding her of something called the Magical Mystery Tour. Sixties stuff, I guessed. Whenever they talked that sort of code, I knew it was about those old days. They are really eighties people, but they just love the sixties, talk about it all the time, the music, the attitude, how cool it must have been. They even use words and sayings from then. Sometimes I feel like they're caught in a time capsule.

The shack was only interesting before you got into it. The door was unlocked, a fact that brought more praise for Newfoundlanders from Dad. But inside it was filthy. You just knew that someone else had been there recently—meaning some time in the past two or three months. And whoever it was hadn't cleaned up properly. There was a sink with dirty dishes still in it and canned food on shelves and mice running around on the floor, which had food stains on it. The smell nearly made me sick. I stepped outside. Inside, Dad was talking to me.

"Cool," he said. "We can get some more grub here." I think he thought he was in the movies at this point. "Dylan, we'll just chow down on what we find and leave some for the next guy. That's the way the world should work."

"I'm not eating any of that food!" I shouted from outside.

"Dylan, don't be a wimp. This is an opportunity, in this distant corner of the world, to break bread with your fellow human beings. Look, there's canned seal meat here…well, maybe we'll pass on…."

But I just left him there and walked up the path towards the bus. I could hear him still talking to me in the distance. He was really getting it going now. Any bread I was going to break was coming from the frozen stuff we bought at Loblaws before we left. *I'll eat the smoked salmon from the cooler and pretend it's seal if that's what he wants.*

When I got to the bus the door was wide open and a stench nearly as bad as in the shack was drifting out. But inside Mom was lying on one of the makeshift bunks.

"I love you," she said and smiled at me.

Gag me.

By the look on her face I could tell she was feeling very, what do they say, groovy, about this bus. Mom the businesswoman had completely disappeared. The way she was feeling was probably a lot like the way Rhett, the Bomb, and I feel when we've got the house to ourselves, TV, laptops, and the whole ball of wax.

"This reminds me of when your dad and I were young," she said. "This is true sharing. Imagine how many people have slept here. People come out here to interact with nature and everyone stays in the same place. It's—"

"Groovy."

"No, I wasn't going to say that...little Mr. Critic. Come on over here and relax. Throw yourself on a bunk and we'll talk."

But as I looked around I felt something strange engulf me. Suddenly I just wanted to get away. And it wasn't that I wouldn't enjoy talking to Mom or being hugged. In fact, a hug and a few words with her wouldn't have been so bad about now. It was just that this bus and that shack were starting to freak me out. Not just the smell and all the unclean people who had wrapped these blankets around themselves, it was more than that. Ireland's Eye was sitting out there on the horizon, with its ghost town just waiting for me. I knew it would be unlike anything I had ever seen and now I was within a morning's paddle. I couldn't sleep in this place that felt like it belonged to others, or eat off plates that seemed abandoned in the night, as if the people who had been sitting here a short while ago had suddenly evaporated into the Newfoundland mists. Many of the citizens who had lived here were dead now, and on these rocks buildings had once stood for centuries. Today, we suddenly appear from the city. We walk where their little village used to be. Everything they had is gone.

There was a presence here and that was the last thing I needed the night before I entered Ireland's Eye. First there had been living jelly bags with faces and then whale-sized fish and then a pterodactyl, and now this. As I stood looking at Mom, the old Newfoundlander's warning sounded clearly in my ears. *Do not go to Ireland's Eye.* "I'm not sleeping here, Mom."

Moments later they found me sitting on the wharf. "Dylan, you shouldn't be afraid," said Dad. "There's nothing here that will hurt you."

"I'm not afraid. I just want to sleep in my own tent and eat my own food. That's all."

I could feel them looking at each other.

That night another dream came, and it was the worst so far. It started out wonderfully. Mom and Dad and I were paddling into Ireland's Eye. The water was calm and even warm when it touched our hands. When we came into the harbour the village was bright and colourful and, miraculously, the streets were filled with people. They were running towards the wharf to greet us and the bells were ringing in the church. But as we approached, something made me look down into the water, and there was the old Newfoundlander coming after me. I shook my head and looked again, expecting to see a red-faced jellyfish. But it was the old man, all right. He shot out of the water like a whale, grabbed the side of my kayak, and flipped it over. Then he jerked me from my cockpit, the spray skirt snapping off like a top from a jar, and started pulling me down into the depths. I kept fighting him and I would wiggle away and get back up to the surface. I screamed to my mom and dad as I hit the air, but they didn't hear me. I saw them moving slowly and calmly towards the wharf. Up came the old man again, grasping my leg and hauling me back underwater. I struggled with everything I had, broke away again and swam to the surface. This time my parents were getting out at the wharf, smiling and shaking hands with people. That was when the old man took me down for the final time. The last thing I remember before I screamed was my grandfather's corpse lying on the bottom of the ocean. It was the first time he had ever been dead in any of my dreams.

"Dylan!" said Mom. "Wake up! You're all right! We're here!"

I stopped screaming and sat up. Dad tried to smile at me. Mom looked grim. Outside, the whales, the eagles, and the ocean were deathly silent.

6

THE MAGICAL ISLAND

All the way through the trip to the Eye the next morning, through the calm first part, the heightening waves, the near-catastrophes, I kept telling myself it was all worthwhile, that what I would see out there would be unforgettable.

The water had been so calm at the beginning and looked so quiet out to the horizon that Mom didn't even question whether or not we should go forward. She watched me carefully but could see that I had forgotten my nightmare and was happy and excited. I put on my dry suit, clipped on my life jacket, and pulled my spray skirt over the watertight cockpit without even a thought of fear.

But just a couple hundred metres out from the shore, even before the waves began to grow, fear came to us in a big way.

Dad and I were paddling close to each other and Mom was a good distance away. We were talking, probably about the Leafs or the Jays, when suddenly he stopped in mid-sentence. I could tell that something was scaring him, and scaring him mightily, but he didn't want to say anything.

"What's wrong, Dad?"

"Nothing."

"Dad, you're scaring me. What's wrong?"

He paused for a moment, as if trying to make a decision, and then spoke quietly. I could tell he didn't want Mom to hear.

"Don't look down."

Of course, I immediately lowered my head. I didn't see anything, just the water, or what appeared to be the water, though it seemed a slightly darker colour than usual.

"It's just water, Dad."

"No, it's not, Dylan."

I peered down again. This time I saw it. An eye twice the size of the minke's was looking at me, and its stare was paralyzing.

"Stay calm," Dad whispered.

"What is it?"

"A fin."

Fin whales make minkes look like minnows. Imagine a fish the size of a Greyhound bus. Then imagine that bus floating a couple of kayak-lengths beneath you in a kilometre of water. He was so immense that I hadn't even noticed him at first. He *was* the water all around us.

For the next five minutes he watched us and we moved forward silently. When Mom smiled over at us, we smiled back. The fin was investigating us, what sort of little insignificant fish we were. And we were hoping he liked us.

It seemed that at any moment he could decide to do us in. We knew whales weren't given to that sort of thing, but the unblinking stare of that clear dark eye frightened us down to the bottom of our dry suits. It was as though he was escorting us out into a world we knew nothing about. After a while, he blinked, as if to say, "Just thought I'd check you out, intruders," and began to drop into the depths. For a few moments we could see him fading beneath us, the eye still staring up. But then he rolled over and vanished, a soundless, magical beast, so ghostlike that the water around us remained undisturbed, as if he had never existed. The only evidence was our pounding hearts.

MOMENTS LATER THE WAVES began to pick up.

We could see them sweeping across the water in front of us, building out of nowhere as the wind got stronger. Soon it seemed they were growing by the minute, rising like foothills, their peaks nearly a metre high. And then they grew even higher. Before we knew it, an ocean storm had us in its grip, attacking us with expanding two-metre waves. We couldn't go back, but going forward seemed terrifying. The storm was all around us, coming from Ireland's Eye and flying towards Random Island. I knew we were in extreme danger. But what lay ahead meant too much to me to give up. I clenched my jaw tightly and crashed forward.

The next hour was the most frightening of my life. The giant waves, the moments of desperation, the conference with Mom and Dad in the cove of the small island where we decided we had no choice but to make a run for it, the gale force strength of the ocean wind as we approached the entrance to Ireland's Eye—all went by in a blur. I gripped my paddle like it was the only thing in the world that was keeping me alive and fixed my gaze straight ahead.

That first sighting of the Eye, the moment when it suddenly went from a shadow to something real, was awesome. It seemed to come up suddenly in the rain and wind to my left, like a magical creature hiding itself until you could see the whites of its eyes. Crashing forward, I glanced up at the rocky shoreline and saw the caribou standing there in the wind, staring out at us. For a second I was amazed that there was actually life on this mysterious island. But I also remember thinking that we might never get near it.

Somewhere behind me, I knew my mother's mind was locked on me, fearing for me and desperately wanting to help, even as she frantically tried to survive herself. I knew she must be consumed by the greatest and most desperate guilt she had ever felt, asking herself what in the world she had been thinking when she agreed to take me along on this unpredictable journey.

Out of the corner of my eye, I noticed Dad churning up beside me. "Don't look at me!" he yelled. "Keep looking straight ahead!" He didn't sound guilty at all. He was intense and on the job with his son in a perilous adventure. In a weird way, I thought, he loves this. He is anxious for me, he is ready to sacrifice whatever he has to for me, but he loves this.

"We are going to turn left and head towards the island!" he shouted. "That's where the town was! That's where we can land! Mom's going in first, then you, and I'll bring up the rear!"

Suddenly Mom darted in front of me and led the way. She didn't even look in my direction. Her jaw was set tightly, her expression grim.

We began turning. In seconds the entrance to the island loomed before us like an escape hatch out of the raging ocean. But at that instant, as if on command from some sort of power stronger than any of us, the storm's anger became awesome. It seemed to be telling us to keep away from the island, warning us to leave it be. The waves turned into mountains so high I could no longer see anything, not Mom or Dad or even Ireland's Eye. A force that felt like a hurricane picked me up and lifted me high into the air. I twisted sideways, my kayak almost above me, desperately out of control. That was when I felt myself going down.

I THOUGHT THAT WAS it, game over. I was about to drown at the entrance to Ireland's Eye. Mom had been right: the trip was too much for a kid. Perhaps what had been pulling me towards this magical island was death itself.

But somewhere up in the air, in that split second that seemed to take hours, I heard my grandfather's voice. It was calm. He told me to get a grip on myself, to think of what I had to do, that I was capable of more than I imagined. He told me to twist the opposite way from the way I was going, and then to let my body go loose. Stiffness would kill me. It struck me that Dad had taught me to react exactly like this during an emergency, but fear had made me forget it. I twisted, I righted myself, I landed, and didn't fight the landing, loosening my body and allowing the kayak to sit flat in the waves.

Then something miraculous happened. The next wave picked me up and shot me forward with great power. But it felt like a friendly push and when I landed everything was calm. I was in the huge old harbour of Ireland's Eye and the world was strangely serene. Mom was ahead of me, floating on still water, her face filled with a smile. Behind me Dad came shooting out of the waves, landing, just like me, in the calm embrace of Ireland's Eye harbour. He was staring backward.

"Look!" he cried.

Fifty metres behind us, in the angry water beyond the harbour, a humpback whale was breaching. Nearly the size of the fin, he came up with ten times the surge of the minke and roared as he flew into the air. He seemed to look our way and then exploded back into the raging ocean.

But here in Ireland's Eye we felt protected from the outside world. Without even mentioning the humpback, Dad and I turned and paddled slowly towards Mom. We were in a magical kingdom. The hills went up on all sides of the old harbour like protective walls, green at their bottoms and rock-grey at the top. They seemed to touch the sky. It was as though a giant hand had reached out and sculpted a perfect harbour, a world unto itself, unseen until you came around that corner and into the tiny opening of Ireland's Eye.

There was absolute silence. We could hear our paddles dipping into the water and see the rings we created going out along the surface from our boats, as if the water hadn't been disturbed for centuries. Even a slight rustling in our cockpits echoed off the walls.

We saw the town in the distance, looking at first like a perfectly normal place. As we drew closer we could see the houses arranged in no particular order from the bottom of the hills to the top, and though some were broken-down, others looked as though someone could step out of the front door and wave hello. Near the top of the hill straight in front of us, the church looked large and stable, the sun glinting off a steeple that still proudly pointed towards heaven. I looked up into the sky and saw an eagle, a speck in the distance.

None of us spoke. I kept waiting for someone to come running down to the dock, but no one did. In the empty windows of some of the old houses I imagined I saw faces, or along the stone roads, horses and carts taking men to and from their businesses, or children running towards the schoolhouse. But everything was silent, as silent as a funeral.

We glided towards the wharf, a sense of awe still making us gape. We bumped into the boards gently and just sat there, staring up at the world around us. Finally Mom spoke. It wasn't in her to joke this time.

"It's beautiful," she said, "but it almost doesn't seem real."

"Oh, it's real all right," said Dad quietly. "What do you think of this, Dylan?"

"Awesome."

"Cool?"

"Way cool."

We had completely forgotten about the storm. We got out of the boats, pulled them well up onto land, tied them down, and got out our provisions.

"Listen," said Mom. We all stopped. "I thought I heard something."

We were quiet again.

"I think it's the storm, from the ocean," said Dad.

All three of us instinctively walked out to the end of the wharf and stared back towards the opening to the harbour. Sure enough, in the distance you could hear the waves, but the sound was very faint. Dad grabbed his binoculars.

"The storm looks worse."

"Should we take some precautions?" asked Mom.

"The storm isn't coming in here," I said. It was a strange thing for me to say with such conviction but somehow I knew it was true. Mom and Dad just nodded in agreement.

We were anxious to walk the crude old rock-filled lanes of the town that wound up the sides of the hills like snakes, to explore all the buildings looming above us, and to climb the peaks and admire the view. But only an hour or two of daylight was left, so we hoisted up the tent and cooked and ate our supper. We didn't talk very much. And we kept hearing noises in the night. They didn't sound like animals.

I tried to keep myself calm by thinking of what I knew about this wonderful island. Dad, of course, had made us memorize about a mile of historical information. Ireland's Eye was first occupied more than three hundred years ago by one man, a planter whose origins were likely English (it was his fellow countrymen who frequented these rich waters in their fishing boats, their eyes ever on the alert for pirates and the unfriendly intentions of the French); but Nicholas Quint moved back to the mainland after a year or so, probably overcome by loneliness and hardship. A century passed and the Eye remained uninhabited. But then families slowly started coming in and putting down roots, leaving old homelands in the British Isles and newer ones on the mainland of Newfoundland. By the 1830s there were thirty-two people and seven houses here, and over the next hundred or more years things kept growing: in 1834 they opened a school, at the turn of the century an Anglican church, and by 1911, just before the First World War, nearly two hundred people lived in Ireland's Eye. And that was just in this village, where we were sleeping tonight. At Black Duck Cove, Ivanhoe, and Traytown, smaller communities had been thriving for some time.

Listening to the eerie sounds in the quiet wilderness outside, it was hard to imagine that so many things had happened on this very ground so long ago. There had been life here but it had vanished, as if gone with the wave of a magician's hand. After Newfoundland joined

Canada in the middle of the twentieth century, good roads and railways, better sanitation, electricity, and all the modern conveniences came to the new province. Ireland's Eye, the little island where Trinity Bay met the Atlantic, had none or few of these things—all it had was hard-working people and children blessed with a world of their own. So, just as they had come a couple of centuries earlier, the people began to leave for the mainland. By the mid-1950s, government programs encouraged residents of outports to resettle in larger, better-serviced communities. People were actually paid to leave their homes, or in some cases to float them on rafts, the beds inside still made, many kilometres to new towns. But it was required that these little places move all at once or at least in great numbers. So, votes were taken. This, of course, caused all sorts of bitterness: those who wanted to stay began resenting neighbours who wanted to go, brothers came to dislike brothers. And sometimes, if only a small number of people remained in a community, the government took away their basic services—some villages even had their post offices closed. So in the end, many residents had no choice. They were forced to go.

Ireland's Eye was in the middle of one of these slow deaths by the late 1950s. It must have been sad to see people leaving, one after the other: some family homes actually floated away while others sat defiant in the shrinking community. One day, of course, they would all give up.

When the 1960s began there were only sixty-four people in Ireland's Eye, in 1966 just thirteen, and a few years later there were none. They disappeared. The word that Dad used was "abandoned": Ireland's Eye was abandoned. Most of the houses, the school, and the church still sat here as if waiting for everyone to come home. You could almost hear people now, snoring away or whispering to each other, happy in their beds in the Newfoundland night.

It took me a while to get settled in my sleeping bag. I kept thinking about the way things must have been here long ago and the pain that people must have felt when their world fell apart. It was so strange, so frightening really, that something like that could happen. It sort of seemed like what had happened to Grandpa: he had been born and had lived his life, and we had all treasured him, but now he was gone as if he had never even been here. That's what happens to all of us, I guess.

I pushed those thoughts aside. But that only made room for others. The raging ocean and my brush with death entered my head at full speed, terrifying moments running through my mind in vivid Technicolor. It seemed that I would never get to sleep. To calm the storm in my head, I tried to focus on the silence outside.

Before long it started to work: slowly a feeling of peace came over me, like a gentle wave from a much kinder ocean. I forgot all the problems that had been racing through my mind and drifted off; the last thing I remember was smiling, enchanted to finally be way out here in the ocean on the magical island that had been filling my imagination for so long. Even though several times I roused a little, thinking I heard footsteps outside the tent, and worrying in those moments that tonight would bring the worst nightmare of the whole trip, I faded into the soundest sleep I had had in a very long time.

7

GHOSTS

When I awoke, the sun was shining through the unzipped tent door and both Mom and Dad were off investigating. There aren't many strange places where they would leave me on my own, but here on Ireland's Eye, other than some small animals and a few friendly caribou (whose ancestors had somehow walked over here on the ice one legendary winter), we were the only living beings within many treacherous kilometres. You could shout at the top of your lungs and no one would hear you. You could take off your clothes and run around naked and no one would say a word. It was a wonderful feeling. The silence was amazing. We were absolutely alone.

Or so it seemed.

I walked out to the end of the dock again with Dad's binoculars. Looking through them I was shocked to see the storm still raging beyond the harbour's entrance. Here on the island it was a beautiful day, almost hot, and the sky was cloudless. In the distance I could see another island, not nearly as big as the Eye, but green and friendly looking. Residents had called Anthony Island "the Garden," because they had planted their vegetables there, unable to grow anything here on these rocks. Every summer day the women would row out there, a couple of kilometres of effort, work in their gardens and come home.

What would the people of Ireland's Eye do on a day like today? And what would they do on a winter day if for some reason they had a desperate need to get to the mainland?

The rest of the world seemed so far away that I imagined there were sea dragons in the ocean, swirling about in those two-metre waves and snapping their tails. I panned away from the entrance, swinging the binoculars around Ireland's Eye, past the houses, the school, up to the church and—for an instant—I thought I saw a face! It passed through the lens quickly. I darted the binoculars back to the window in the church steeple.

I could have sworn that just a split second ago a man's face had been staring out at me…but if indeed he had ever been there, he was gone now.

I had to be imagining things.

"Dylan! Dylan! Up here!" I turned in the direction of the voice. It was Mom. She and Dad were almost directly above me, stepping carefully along some tricky rock paths, holding hands to keep each other from falling. (They're hand-holders, the parental units.) They were way up at the top of a rugged hill and had come to a spot that used to be someone's backyard. "You can see everything from here! Come on!" yelled Mom. She sounded excited.

Five minutes later, huffing and puffing, I was beside them. I had followed one of those steep village pathways myself, probably used as a road in the old days. It was bedded with huge rocks the men had somehow carried up or down the mountainous hills. And here I was at the top of their cliff, out of breath just from climbing.

But what a reward you got from putting the effort into getting here. Looking out you could see the whole sweep of the little bay, the ocean in the distance, all the homes, the school, and the church.

A big house, probably the biggest in the village, sat silently next to us. Mom and Dad had been into a few homes, but had waited for me to climb up before venturing into this one. We walked around to the front door. Mom knocked.

When we pushed on the door it creaked open like something from a horror show. Inside everything was strangely in place.

"Groovy," said Dad, and then looked a little apologetically at me.

"All the other ones were empty, but look at this!" said Mom, moving towards the kitchen. "Watch your step, Dylan, some of the boards are rotten."

The rugs were still on the living room floor, dressers remained in place, couches sat as they had been left and a calendar, turned to December 1959, was pinned to a wall. Up in the ceiling corners, along the window edges and even stretched between furniture and the walls were massive spider webs, traps waiting to entangle their prey. Dust sat on things like snow. There was an overpowering smell of mould and something stale, like the still-lingering smoke from an ancient wood stove.

"This is a defiant house," said Dad with admiration. "Whoever lived here must have vowed to leave it the way it was."

It was the pick of the homes in the town. When we rubbed away some dirt from the big picture windows downstairs and the smaller ones in the upstairs bedrooms, the view was magnificent. I started thinking the mayor must have lived here, or at least the town leader. In fact, "the mayor's house" struck me as a good name for this home, so from then on that's what I called it.

There were four rooms upstairs. One was obviously the master bedroom, so it didn't interest me. I picked out another that had certainly belonged to a kid. The door was slightly ajar and as I put my hand up to it the strangest thing happened: it slowly swung open on its own. I could have sworn I hadn't touched it, but I must have. I stood back for a second, collected myself, and entered. I think my eyeballs went in first, then my nose, then the rest of me. Looking down to check for bad wood, I saw a small clump of dirt about the size of a dime on the floor near the entrance. It looked dark and wet. *That's odd*, I thought, and then pushed it from my mind.

The bed was made. Just above a night table, pinned to the wall with a rusty thumbtack, was a cardboard colour photograph of the bruising Gordie Howe taken from the back of a cereal box. "Mr. Hockey" stood smiling out at the camera, looking innocent of all charges.

Something made me want to sit on the kid's bed. Slowly I lowered myself, easing down, afraid the frame might suddenly collapse. But it didn't move an inch. It felt good just to rest here for a minute. I relaxed, swung my legs up and stretched out. Soon I was lying there imagining what it must have been like to grow up on Ireland's Eye.

Where did they play hockey? Were they able to get NHL games even without electricity? Maybe they had transistor radios.

I closed my eyes and heard the hockey game coming faintly through a little battery-operated radio on a winter's day in the 1950s, static clouding the reception. Perhaps the boy had it tucked under his pillow so his parents wouldn't know he was still awake. I thought of Grandpa's descriptions of those great long-gone players, and of the voice of Foster Hewitt calling the play as he sat in the gondola at Maple Leaf Gardens in Toronto. I thought of the boy lying here, the lights out and the game crackling through the pillow. Outside the wind howls and the waves break against the shore.

Perhaps he's listening to the Leafs and the Canadiens, hearing Hewitt describe the moves of Rocket Richard and Grandpa's favourite, Teeder Kennedy, tall and strong, playing for the love of the game, a captain of captains. Perhaps it is April 21, 1951, overtime at the Gardens, fifth game of the Stanley Cup final. Every match in the series has gone into extra periods, the Rocket potting the winner in game two, Teeder burying the Habs the next night at the Forum. But now, the Leafs can win it all. The whole nation is listening and so am I, a boy living on Ireland's Eye. Bill Barilko, "Billy the Kid," a young defenceman who was supposed to stay in position at the blueline, decides to take a chance. Out here on this island in the ocean, I'm listening to the shouts of the crowd. My mind is full of images of things I have never seen. What would it look like? Is Teeder out there now? How heroic does he look? Is he tending to his defensive duties? Is he looking up to find the Rocket as he sees young Barilko leave his position? Does he even bother to look behind him? Does Barilko hear the roar of the crowd like I do? He's spotted a loose puck. He grabs it, swoops past the left faceoff dot and fires a dart, falling as he does. The Montreal goalie, Gerry McNeil, taken by surprise, stumbles as he scrambles to recover and…it's in! IT'S IN! THE LEAFS HAVE WON THE STANLEY CUP! THEY'VE BEATEN THE CANADIENS AT MAPLE LEAF GARDENS! THE WHOLE NATION IS LISTENING! THE CROWD IS GOING WILD!

"Dylan? What are you shouting about? Are you all right?"

"Fine. It's nothing."

I fixed my eyes on the picture of Gordie Howe. When I was little I actually saw him a few times on TV looking old and friendly, very unlike the big bruiser Grandpa always talked about. But in this picture he looks the part, young and ready, arms bulging through his sweater, legs as thick as pillars. It occurred to me that the boy who lived here and pinned that picture to the wall had aged too; it's possible that he's not even alive anymore.

Looking out through his bedroom window I could see the whole harbour and it seemed like a painting. What a place to live!

Mom and Dad were calling again. They wanted to get moving and explore more of the island, but I was reluctant to leave. For some reason it felt like the boy had never left here, as though he were just out trading hockey cards with someone, or down in the schoolyard. But he had gone on in life to adventures and ups and downs I couldn't even imagine.

That bedroom was a wonderful place.

At least it was until I stood up and began moving towards the hallway. That was when I saw something that chilled me to the bone.

There on the dresser was a cigarette—a *burning* cigarette! For a minute I just stood there staring at it. *A burning cigarette, in here!* I walked over to it, picked it up, and put it out. Then, with my heart pounding, I set it down again and descended the stairs. I didn't say a word to Mom and Dad.

They were still in a happy mood and noticed right away that I wasn't. I saw worried looks on their faces that I hadn't seen since before we entered the harbour of Ireland's Eye. Mom was kind of looking at Dad and he was trying to look away; they both kept glancing at me. But I couldn't speak and I couldn't bring myself to be happy. We walked out into the backyard and worked our way into the low-lying marshy area behind the town that led to the schoolhouse.

Why was a lighted cigarette sitting in that room?

Were there ghosts on Ireland's Eye? Was someone watching us, some creature, or some half-crazed person who had stayed behind, alone for fifty years on this island in the ocean? Was there any reasonable explanation?

How could a cigarette light itself? I thought for a few minutes, my mind racing, fear making me confused. *How can a cigarette light itself?*

Then it dawned on me that there actually *were* ways. What if the boy had had a magnifying glass sitting somewhere between the window and the cigarette? A day with an intense sun could light it, couldn't it? Then I realized why I had thought of the magnifying glass in the first place—because I had seen one! And it had been sitting near the window too, curiously left propped up on its side. *That must be it!* I started feeling better.

But I was clutching at straws and I knew it. Imagine how long it would have to have been there. Thirty years or more! A cigarette had been sitting there for fifty years and it was only *now* that it had caught fire! That couldn't be the answer. A wave of terror came over me again.

I kept trudging beside my parents, almost ready to cry, my face burning with fear. I remembered what I had heard Grandpa saying to me when I was in trouble at the entrance to Ireland's Eye. *Stay calm. Think.* Was there any other explanation?

The fact that we planned a trip to Ireland's Eye must mean that others come here too. Maybe someone was here recently and left a cigarette on the dresser, and the magnifying glass or some other natural process caused it to light itself. There are so many cloudy days in Newfoundland that there might only be one sunny day for months on end. Surely someone has been here sometime this whole summer! I kept thinking about that magnifying glass sitting on its side. Sure it would be a fluke, and a big one, but it's a possibility isn't it?

I wasn't convinced. But I vowed to stop thinking about it. Mom says there are too many "negative vibes" in the world anyway and that if people thought positively, life would *be* more positive. For once I decided to take her advice.

"I'll race you!" I cried out and tore off across the swamp towards the schoolhouse. Mom and Dad hesitated, looking at each other, surprised. Then they ran after me, laughing. I think Mom laughed the loudest.

The swamp was the only large flat piece of land in the town. It sat behind the buildings and was surrounded by trees that went up the far slope of the hill and blocked any view of the other side of the island. It was about the size of two football fields, but no one could have played any kind of ball on this swampy land. People must have invented their own games on the steep rocky hills in town. Maybe in the winter the marsh froze. Now there's a thought—what a hockey rink! But what if they played on the bay and the whole town watched from their windows?

At the other end of the swamp land we climbed a steep embankment up to the schoolhouse. There wasn't much room here so we walked around to the other side. The big front door, with a rusty old bell above it, was boarded shut. We moved to the broken windows, but they were too high to look through.

"Here, Dylan," said Dad, "I'll give you a boost."

I put a foot, soaking wet from our swamp march, into his clasped hands and then felt myself going up along the wooden wall. Slowly the classroom, single and huge, came into view. There were toppled desks, a blackboard at the front, a broken globe lying on the floor, and a little cloakroom at the back. But what really got me was what I saw through the long windows on the other side of the room. They seemed to go nearly from the ceiling to the floor and out through them you could see the swamp land and then the trees on the hills in the distance. They filled the whole space. In my school at home all you saw through the small windows of most classes was a wall, though through one or two you could see a McDonald's and some other stores. I looked out at the trees and the blue sky and imagined sitting here in class seeing *that* outside!

"Dad! Boost me all the way up."

Another shove and I was in, landing on top of a desk. I slipped and fell into it and found myself sitting there as if I were in class.

"Be careful!" I could hear Mom shouting.

But I wasn't listening, for I was suddenly back in time, long before Mom was even born. At the front of the class the teacher seemed to be wearing a costume, her dress flowing down to the floor, and the children all leaned forward working at something on their desks. There were small boys and girls and teenagers who looked almost like adults. They were flesh and blood just like me, some looking neat and tidy and others dirty, with their hair messed. I could have given them clothes like mine and taken them back to Toronto with me and no one would ever have known that they were really people who had lived long ago, people perhaps my grandfather's age or even older.

I sat at the back and raised my head, looking out through those windows. The sun was gleaming in, leaving squares of sunlight on our backs, and we could hear the birds singing and the water lapping against the shore. Men were shouting as they put their boats into the harbour and mothers were calling out to each other as they worked in their back yards. I wondered what we would all do for fun when the bell rang. Then I remembered that I was the only one not paying attention to my work.

"DYLAN!"

"Yes, ma'am."

"Are you going deaf in your advanced years?" asked Dad.

"What did you call me?" asked Mom.

"Nothing."

"Good answer. Not a truthful one, mind you."

"Mrs. Nothing and I would like to know what you see in there? Would that be possible?"

"It's really neat," I said, walking carefully towards the front of the class, for some reason picking up desks as I went.

"And…"

"Well, it's like a real classroom. It's like they were using it just a few weeks ago or something."

"Are there any maps or papers around?"

"There's a globe, but it's busted. Oh…" I had looked up and noticed for the first time a large roll-down map nailed to a wall and hanging over an old blackboard near the front of the class. It was so dusty that it looked almost the colour of the wall.

"There's a bigger one too."

"Look at Newfoundland. Is it the same colour as the rest of Canada?"

I walked over and rubbed off some of the dust.

"Uh…no."

"It was made before 1949, then."

Before 1949, I thought, as I walked back into the centre of the room and started running my hands along the initials carved into the desks. Before Barilko scored, before Mom and Dad existed, when Grandpa was young, before Newfoundland was even a part of Canada.

I remembered the story that Grandpa always told about Bill Barilko. After he scored that goal, Billy the Kid went on a fishing trip to northern Ontario, all the way up to Hudson Bay, and the plane crashed and he was killed. The last thing he ever did on the ice was score the winning goal in the Stanley Cup final against the Montreal Canadiens in overtime at Maple Leaf Gardens! But that wasn't the whole story. They were unable to find the plane for many years and a legend grew that the Leafs would never again win the Cup until the dashing young defenceman's body was found. From 1951 to 1961 they didn't even come close. It was said that the ghost of Barilko haunted the Gardens. Then, in the spring of 1962, the Leafs became champions again.... Two months later his bones were found deep in the northern bush.

"Dylan, what else do you see?"

"Uh...uh...not much." I moved slowly into the cloakroom and peered carefully around the corner.

Perhaps there would be a boy's coat or an old pair of boots inside. But it was empty. I decided to walk back to the window where Mom and Dad were waiting. As I came down an aisle I noticed that one desk, the only one that had been sitting perfectly upright when I came in, had what appeared to be a series of letters carved into it. As I approached I noticed that it was more than just initials; when I came right up to it I realized that *my own name* was staring back at me, carved deeply into the desktop!

It looked fresh, as though someone had cut it in that very day. I ran my fingers along it and as I did a loud noise came from the front of the room. I whirled around in time to see the big map snapping up. Dust flew off it, creating a thick fog. I stood there, shaking, waiting to see if anyone or anything appeared once the dust settled. But there was nothing except the blackboard and specks glowing like gold in the rays of sun as the dust moved towards me.

"What was that?" asked Mom.

"Nothing," I said quickly.

As I climbed down from the school window into Dad's arms my mind was full of questions. How could that map suddenly roll up on its own? Was someone watching me all the time I was in the school? Who?

What? Why was my name carved on the one desk that was standing? Why did it look like it had been done recently?

As we started walking away, Mom was a few strides ahead. I hung back with my father.

"Dad?"

"Yes, sir?"

"Was Dylan a common name around here a long time ago?" '

"Why do you ask?"

"No reason."

"The name Dylan? I doubt it. It's been popular since the sixties."

I didn't ask why. I didn't care, frankly. I just wished he had said that it was popular all over Newfoundland for as long as anyone can remember, that just about every kid who had sat in that school would have been named Dylan…and that there was a good reason why my name was freshly carved in a desk.

I must have just imagined it.

"Let's go up to the church!" cried Mom, far ahead of us by now and unaware that my mood had changed again.

Dad knew differently. He turned his head sideways and looked into my eyes, which were directed at the ground….

"Something you want to talk about?"

"No."

"You sure?"

"Yeah."

"Look, I know it can be a little spooky here, but it's a ghost town, remember? I thought that's why you wanted to come. There's often a little danger in any good adventure."

He was probably right. What drew me to the island was what was scaring me now. It was mysterious and dangerous out here, but I'd wanted that, hadn't I? And there were probably good explanations for all of these scary things. I just hadn't figured them out yet.

"I've got an idea," said Dad. "Let's get some grub first, kick back a little. Then we'll go up and explore the church. How's that sound, buddy?"

He must really be worried about me. He hasn't called me "buddy" in years. But I didn't say anything. He shouted for Mom and she stopped and came back from the spot she had gotten to, about halfway up the rocks towards the church. She looked a little surprised at the change of plans, suspicious in fact, her eyes searching Dad's face. But he was a great poker player. He didn't betray any of my fears. He just made another crack about grub and kicking back and got her to laugh. He put his arm around her and we descended to our tent and made our meal.

I did my best not to seem freaked out. But I found myself pacing around, looking over at the mayor's house and the school, sometimes actually believing that I saw more faces in the windows. I even started walking while I was eating, until Dad very smoothly drew me down to a spot near the fire and started talking about a nice pass I had made to Rhett Norton the last game we'd played. "Relax," he whispered to me as he stood to go down to the water to clean his plate. He had turned his head so Mom couldn't see his mouth move.

I tried to. I took my plate, followed him, and squatted down beside him. Dad and I were in the same boat, so to speak. We both wanted to stay here and we both knew that in order to do that we had to hide my fears from Mom. But if I told him what I'd seen in the kid's room and the schoolhouse, he might get me out of here as fast as Mom. So I had to keep it from him too. It looked like I was going to have to gut this one out and solve these weird problems for myself.

Dad leaned over and whispered to me again, "Uh, you don't have to wash your serviette, Dylan. They're, uh, made of paper." I looked down and saw that mine, held firmly between my two tight fists in the water, was torn to bits and floating away in soggy little pieces. "Smile at your mom when you stand," he said. I did. She smiled back.

"Look," he continued, still under his breath and facing the ocean, "we're going to the church next. How scary can that be? There's nothing here to be frightened about, believe me. You've just let yourself get worked up. You'll be okay."

Nothing to be frightened of? I sure hoped he was right. I looked up and saw the church looming on the hill.

We didn't go to church back home. Mom and Dad gave up religion in university and brought me up to take a scientific approach to things. They encouraged me to have what they called spirituality in my life, but I'd never really figured out what that was. Every religion but Christianity was discussed in our house.

But Dad was probably right again. How scary *can* a church be? Even if you don't believe, there's something comforting in being in a place where people go to pray. So up the hill we went towards it, Mom starting out fast and scampering way ahead of us, Dad second, turning around to see me from time to time as I brought up the rear.

All of the town, other than the landing area and the swamp land, was steep. But the steepness varied. In places it flattened out a little, while in others you felt like you were scaling Mount Everest. The church sat on the rocks at the highest point in the town and getting to it required the skill of a mountain goat. My fear soon lessened as I concentrated on finding the right ridges in the rocks to set my feet on. How in the world did they ever get to church in the old days? Perhaps they flew up here.

The view at the entrance to the church was at least as good as at the mayor's house. Tired from our climb, we sat on the front steps and looked out over Ireland's Eye. I imagined the minister or the priest or whatever he was, standing here watching people make their way up the hill towards him, with the bell tolling above. The whole town would look like an anthill, with ants swarming towards him. And anyone who wasn't coming to church could easily be spotted.

Suddenly the bell sounded.

"Wind," said Mom, looking my way.

"Wind," repeated Dad, nodding at me as if I was supposed to nod back.

But the church wasn't scary at all, just as Dad had predicted. Inside its walls my fear faded even more. It almost seemed to float away. I think Mom and Dad were comforted by the church, too, though they didn't let on.

We walked through the entrance and closed the door and everything was silent. Had it not been for the peeling walls, the broken stained glass and the absence of pews, we might have been in a church back home. Straight in front of us at the other end of the building was a large cross, looking like a plus sign standing tall in the wreckage. On my way towards it I stumbled over something metallic. It was a plaque honouring church members who had died in wars going back a hundred years.

If I had lived here, I would have just let those wars be. Let people in the rest of the world hurt each other if they had to, over disagreements that would come and go. They fought because of things like money or oil or prejudice, over who they thought God was or where a border should be marked, killing each other to make everything right. But here in Ireland's Eye that all seemed so far away.

To the left of the cross was the place where the minister preached and it looked like it had hardly changed. You walked up a set of stairs and stood inside a circular cubicle that came up to your waist. Your notes rested in front of you. Climbing the stairs, I imagined the minister doing the same, looking down at his people and out through the window at the beautiful harbour. I imagined him praying for men who had gone away to fight in wars on battlefields the townspeople would never see, in the world that lay beyond the entrance to Ireland's Eye.

Standing where the minister stood gave me a feeling of power. I looked down at my parents and smiled. As I did I stepped forward a little and my knee brushed against something. Leaning down, I was surprised to find a huge black bible. I lifted it up, set it on the rest in front of me and blew off the dust. "Ireland's Eye Church, 1901," read the inscription on the front page. I opened it, searching for a sentence I might boom out in the church to startle my parents and make me feel like a real preacher. I noticed some passages were underlined. I rejected a few and then found one.

"Blessed are those who mourn," I read, my voice echoing in the church as I tried to sound ominous, "for they shall be comforted."

"Dylan, I don't think you should be doing that," said Mom. There wasn't even a hint of a smile on her face. I closed the Bible with a thud and dust went flying up. Then I very gingerly returned it to its spot, as if the lesson for the day was over. I have to admit, I was feeling a little smart-alecky. I suppose you get that way when you go from petrified to normal to petrified and back again every few minutes or so.

"Let's climb the bell tower," Mom said, giving me a bit of a look, as if she wondered what the heck was going on between my ears. Exercise was one of her ways of solving problems. At home, she'd run when she was feeling stressed out, as she put it. And here in the church she had spotted an entrance with a busted-in door, off to my right down below the pulpit. She could see that it led upward and the only thing above us was the bell tower. We entered and edged slowly up the winding stairs, each step creaking. By the time we reached the top we were all puffing a little but the view was magnificent, unquestionably the best in Ireland's Eye. Luckily, Dad had brought his binoculars. He scanned the whole harbour and the gap out into the Atlantic.

"Still stormy out there," he said. "I can't understand it. Kind of gives you the willies."

Mom took a turn with the binoculars for a while and then they were handed to me. I looked at the gap, the mayor's place, peered into the schoolhouse, the swamp, and then down at our boats. I kept seeing things. In the mayor's house I thought I saw shadows moving, and near the kayaks in the long grass someone seemed to be lying flat on the ground as if hiding, looking up towards us in the church. But the weirdest thing was something I couldn't confirm—on my second scan of the schoolhouse, I leaned out of the tower to see as much of the front of the classroom as I could and thought I saw the edge of the big map, the one that had rolled up so loudly when I was near it. *It looked to me like it was rolled down again!*

"Hey!" Mom yelled, pulling me back into the tower. "What's so fascinating that it's worth falling to your death?"

"Nothing."

I couldn't be sure about the map. I hadn't seen it clearly enough. So as I walked down the steep creaky stairs of the church tower I tried not to jump to any more conclusions.

"Where to next?" Dad asked.

"How about the graveyard?" said Mom.

8

TERROR IN THE GRAVEYARD

Mom and Dad had read that there was a graveyard on Ireland's Eye. The guidebook wasn't very clear about where it was, just noted that it existed and that it was somewhere behind the church, not far off a path that led up over the very top of the hill to the other side of the island. If you descended on that side you came to another abandoned village, a much smaller one called Black Duck Cove. It sounded pretty creepy to me.

So did exploring a graveyard. It wasn't exactly my first choice for our next adventure, but Mom was getting her dark sense of humour back and wanted us to have our picnic there later on, so off we went. We found a path marked by rocks and very unlike anything anyone would choose to walk along—it was grown over and difficult to follow. It led straight into the woods and was even less recognizable once we got in there. But we stuck to a line where just small bushes and little trees grew amongst the bigger ones, and assumed that this must be what we were looking for. Before long we were reaching the crest of the hill and walking on rough but fairly flat land, with the woods thick all around us. It was a strange feeling. We were in a place that could have been near our cottage back home, yet we were miles from civilization, on Ireland's Eye.

The sun was getting lower in the sky, its rays playing off the leaves, creating a strange glowing light in the woods. Daydreaming, I stared off at things—an old stump here, a fallen tree there—and before long was lagging behind. A few minutes later I looked up to say something to Mom and Dad and realized that I couldn't even see them...anywhere. Panicking, I began to run, searching for glimpses of their white T-shirts in front of me, listening for their voices. I saw something glint, a sudden metallic flash in the trees, but it wasn't them. My breathing got heavier and my heart started to pound.

As I rushed about I wasn't paying attention to the treacherous ground beneath me and seconds later my foot caught on something and I fell. Instantly I was face down in the woods. But the feeling against my cheek wasn't like the warm dirt of the earth or the tickle of pine needles—it was cold, clammy, and very hard. I pushed myself up onto my elbows and looked at what I was lying on. It was an overturned tombstone.

"Aaaaahhhh!"

Mom and Dad came running towards me, dodging trees and jumping over dead stumps, until they stood above me. But by the time they arrived I was on my knees, looking very embarrassed.

"It's nothing."

"No, it isn't, Dylan," said Dad excitedly. "It's not nothing at all. It's the graveyard. You've found the graveyard!"

And so I had, though I would have appreciated Dad's sympathy a little more than his glee. Mom smiled at me and gave me a hug. There was motherly comfort in it, which I eagerly accepted. Sometimes you just have to be a kid.

"Look," said Dad, still excited and quickly taking in everything around him. "You must have tripped on the fence. It's lying flat all along here...but look into the woods. It's still standing in there. We must be right on the fence line. I bet we could follow the whole outline of the graveyard if we wanted to!"

It had been a white picket fence. That was obvious from the bits of paint that had survived. It was a very strange sight. The fence went off into the middle of the woods, and a few feet away a rusted gate lay twisted, mangled by everything that had grown through it and around it. In among the trees you could see tombstones, some standing, others lying flat. They were tall thin slabs, rounded off at the top like the arches of church doors, perfectly cut by the hands of craftsmen. In their day they must have been white, but now many looked grey and ancient. The woods hung over everything like a ceiling and seemed to surround the tombstones, pushing them down and crowding them out as they tried to stay upright; moss grew over their surfaces in the wet, salty air. Here and there a wooden cross stood, weather-beaten and rotting. On the stones the carved words were deeply cut and written with great, flowing letters. They were blackened by the years and looked ominous.

I stood there in the dimming light with my mouth wide open. This was the final resting spot for the citizens of Ireland's Eye. There were corpses under the ground all around us. Talk about the willies!

Death was scary enough on its own, but imagine being left behind here in the cold ground out in the Atlantic Ocean, while everyone else deserted the place and went away to the mainland. And yet it seemed sort of peaceful too. Lying face down on the tombstone in the silence of these woods I had felt an instant of peace. That is, until I got up and actually read the inscription.

William Snow,
Beloved Son of Elijah and Ruth Snow,
dead this summer day in the year of our Lord 1899,
age thirteen years, seven months, and two days.
May God bless him and keep him,
may his soul live forever.

It had taken me exactly one second to calculate that *I* was thirteen years, seven months, and *one* day old on *this* summer day—*one* day younger than William Snow!

"Tomorrow," I told myself, totally freaking out. "What the *hell* happens tomorrow?!"

Out loud I said something else: "Let's get out of here." My voice was shaky.

"But it's a lovely graveyard," said Mom, making a desperate attempt at humour.

"No, it's not. It's not *lovely* at all! And I don't mean

we should just get out of *here*, I mean the *hell* out of Ireland's Eye!"

With that I ran from the cemetery, along the path and out of the woods, past the church, down the steep hill, and all the way to the wharf.

Five minutes later my parents found me there, sitting in near darkness, dangling my legs over the water and fighting back tears, staring out at the opening to the harbour.

"What's the matter, Dylan? Tell me." It was Mom. She sounded truly frightened for me. Dad bent over and put a hand on my shoulder.

I spilled my guts. I couldn't hold it in anymore. I told them about the things I had seen. The face in the church steeple, the lighted cigarette, my name carved on the desk, the roll-down map that went up and down on its own, the man in the grass near the kayaks, and finally the tombstone, that horrible tombstone.

I guess they could have argued about my situation, Mom telling Dad that she had told him so. And Dad could have told both of us to quit being wimps and get with the program. But instead they helped me, together. Like I've said, they're pretty annoying at times, and wrapped up in their own worlds, but they usually come through in the crunch.

"Dylan," said Dad, "I think you've been imagining things and I think you've also attached a little too much significance to a couple of coincidences, but I tell you what we'll do. We'll leave. It's too late to go today, but we'll pack everything up tonight and be gone at the crack of dawn in the morning. There's no sense in having you terrified. That isn't much of a holiday." Then he gave me a hug. Mom smiled at both of us and gave Dad a hug.

I started to calm down. The best of all possible plans would have been to leave today, since tomorrow, whether it be the crack of dawn or midnight, was still the day when I would be *exactly* the same age poor William Snow had been when he died. But I tried not to think about that. Dad was probably right again. I was likely imagining things and getting worked up about a few simple coincidences. By the time the sun was halfway up in the sky we would be gone from Ireland's Eye.

I looked out at the entrance. It was still storming.

9

A NIGHT TO REMEMBER

That was the night I had the worst dream of the trip. It started out in the strangest way: I woke up.

I had been dozing in my sleeping bag in the tent between Mom and Dad when I thought I heard a voice. I sat up and listened. The sound was coming from outside. I rose rather noisily, I thought, and even tripped and stumbled over Mom as I moved towards the door. But neither she nor Dad stirred. They looked so stone-cold asleep they could have been dead.

I pulled on my clothes and cautiously unzipped the tent flap. When I peered out I saw a man sitting at a blazing fire warming himself. He was leaning forward so he was almost in the flames, but he kept rubbing his hands as if he couldn't get rid of a chill.

"Hi, Dylan," he said without looking at me.

He was a young man, perhaps twenty-one, handsome and robust. He wore a Toronto Maple Leafs sweater with number 5 on the back.

"They want you up in the graveyard," he said.

"Who are you?"

"Dylan!" said my grandfather. "Don't ask stupid questions. They want you up in the graveyard, now. Get going!"

"But you're so young, Grandpa."

"Do you really think I was always an old coot?" There was anger in his voice. "Give me more credit than that. Look at yourself—I'm younger than you now."

He was right. I gazed down at my hands and saw the wrinkles and liver spots of old age.

"It is just time that makes us young or old," said Grandpa. "Don't judge me by time. I have always been the same person. I laughed and I cried just the same when I was a child as when I was an old man. It was just time you were worried about; time made you judge me."

"But...."

"The graveyard, Dylan! Don't worry, I'll be here when you get back. I'll always be here…as long as you care about me."

I couldn't move. I stood frozen in place looking at my grandfather. Nothing could make me go back to that graveyard, not even him. Why was I *wanted* there? What could that mean? As I stood there I noticed something strange about his eyes, and as I stared into them I realized I could see past the pupils and irises, into a moving picture of the two of us sitting side by side on a Saturday night back home, laughing together as he told me old stories. Slowly I felt myself turning around like a zombie. Then some sort of weird unseen force started pushing me up the hill towards the graveyard.

About halfway to the church my body began transforming, turning back into a kid's. After that my pace picked up and before long I was climbing rapidly. Only the moon lit my way and I had to pick my steps carefully. At the church I turned and looked down at Ireland's Eye. Our tent was there, the kayaks nearby, and Grandpa was still sitting by the fire trying to get his hands warm. He was standing guard, it seemed, over his son and daughter-in-law. I thought of him holding my father in his arms long ago, a little baby smiling up at him, helpless and trusting.

When I reached the woods I couldn't see more than a metre in front of me. Suddenly, just like earlier in the day, I stumbled and fell face down on the ground.

"Get off of me!" said a boy's voice.

That didn't take long, let me tell you. I leapt to my feet, quivering like a sail in the wind.

He stood up the instant I got off of him. He was dressed in dark thick pants held up by suspenders, a heavy navy blue shirt with the sleeves rolled up, and boots like I had seen fishermen wearing in old pictures of Newfoundland. He was about my height and remarkably like me in appearance, with unruly dark hair, dark eyes, and a long straight nose. But he was deathly pale and as thin as a corpse. He reached out and put a hand on my shoulder.... It felt cold right through my clothing.

"You look like you've seen a ghost, Dylan. Relax. My name's William Snow and I'm pleased to make your acquaintance. It gets lonely out here, you know. How are the Leafs doing?"

"But...but...you're dead."

"That's a lovely thing to say."

"But...you are."

"In a manner of speaking. Dead, as you put it, since 1899. That's before the Leafs existed, so you see I've had a few updates. Eavesdropped on a tourist or two, I'll admit. Last time was in the sixties, it seems to me."

He stood close to me, uncomfortably close, staring right into my eyes. His own looked anxious and he was rattling on at an incredible speed, his hands moving as he talked, as if he were trying to tell me everything he knew in an instant, as if he were frantic to keep me right there beside him, talking about something he loved.

"The best team in the world in my day was the Montreal Shamrocks, Stanley Cup champions the spring I died, though the mighty Ottawa Silver Seven were about to get it cranked up. Then came the fabulous Wanderers, out of Montreal too. Great clubs, tough as nails. That was before the *bleu, blanc, et rouge* existed— you know, *Les Glorieux.* Why no Habs until 1910? They didn't figure French Canadians had much interest in the game. Ever heard of Russell Bowie? Harry Trihey? Frank McGee?"

"My grandfather talked about Frank McGee."

"He's a good man, your grandfather."

"Yes, he is…or was."

"Is," said William Snow bluntly. "And what did your grandfather tell you about Frank McGee? Do you remember anything, or was it all just going in one ear and out the other? Do you figure that Frank McGee's whole life can be tossed away and forgotten just because he's dead as far as you know?" He almost sounded angry.

"Frank McGee scored fourteen goals in a single Stanley Cup game in 1905," I blurted out, "a record that stands to this day. When he died in Flanders Fields during the First World War they discovered that he only had one good eye."

"Correct, living boy! I'd like to see Gordie Howe pot fourteen big ones half blind."

"Howe's retired now. Has been for some time, actually. In fact—"

"Oh," he said, screeching to a halt. He seemed a little embarrassed and looked suddenly unhappy.

"Sidney Crosby or Jonathan Toews ring a bell?" I asked.

"No. I…uh…haven't heard of them."

"They're Canadians, but the Russians, the Swedes, and even the Americans are just about as good as us now."

"Sorry to hear that. Makes me glad I'm dead," he tried to laugh. It was sort of like one of Mom's jokes.

"What's that like?"

"Being dead?" The subject seemed to rouse him a little, but he was still speaking more quietly than before. "Oh, it's not so bad, though I'd prefer to be alive. Biggest problem is worrying about being forgotten. It just kind of eats you up. Your grandfather's told you that though, hasn't he?"

"Every night when I go to sleep. And tonight he told me to come up here. Said they wanted me in the graveyard."

"He did?" The boy seemed alarmed.

"What does that mean?"

"Nothing."

"I know it means *something,* something important. Tell me."

The boy looked down, shuffled his feet, and seemed lost in a battle with himself. "I suppose it will come out some time anyway. Ghosts are sworn to tell the truth."

"So tell me."

"It's something bad."

"How bad?"

"Very bad."

"Tell me." I swallowed hard and listened.

"It means…usually…that you're going to—"

"Tell me!"

"Die."

And that was when I really woke up. William Snow vanished from less than a metre in front of me and I found myself standing alone in the woods in the graveyard of Ireland's Eye. It was dark out, and if there was a moon it wasn't giving off any light. I was shivering in my pajamas, absolutely petrified. I had never walked in my sleep before. I raised my arm, brought my watch up close to my face, and looked at the time. It was one minute past midnight.

I had also never screamed before. At least not that I could remember. The scream I released at that moment seemed to come from the soles of my bare feet and go up through my whole body before it escaped from my mouth, like a rocket launched into the night. I screamed for my parents; I screamed for my grandfather and Bill Barilko; I screamed for home and for my teammates and my bedroom and warmth and a world with no ghosts and no mysteries and no Ireland's Eye.

By the time I hit the fourth or fifth scream I was coming to my senses. I started turning back towards the church and running. But as I did, I thought I could hear a voice. It sounded like a young boy's.

"Everything will be all right," I heard him say, but I kept running.

Then he, or something, seemed to be after me. I could hear it rushing through the woods across the cemetery, coming at a run much faster than me. In the distance, at the bottom of the hill, I could hear Mom and Dad calling out, running up towards the church. I called back to them, desperate. But the boy kept coming.

"Everything will be all right, you must know that."

Something told me I had to face this. Something was saying that *this* was what I had come to Ireland's Eye to see. *This* was what had been drawing me ever since Dad first mentioned the island's name that fateful day last year at our cottage. I stopped.

I turned.

Standing about fifty metres behind me I saw a young boy about my age, dressed in tattered clothes. They looked like the remnants of a shirt and pants from another time, maybe a hundred years ago. He had dodged behind a tree when I stopped. Now he peered over a branch at me, looking kindly into my eyes for a second or two. It may have been just my imagination, but I thought he looked like William Snow. Over his shoulder, in the woods, I saw that metallic glint again, flashing and disappearing. The boy seemed to glance at it and then looked back at me mournfully. Then he turned and fled.

I was at the edge of the woods when we locked eyes. Now I stood there like a pillar of salt, frozen in time. But soon I heard Mom and Dad coming up the path towards me. They led me back down to the tent, fed me hot chocolate, and calmed me.

I never told them about what I'd seen.

10

VILLAINS

True to their word, my parents aimed for a crack-of-dawn launching. After my night's adventure they didn't need any more convincing that the time had come to leave Ireland's Eye. We started dismantling the tent and packing before the sun rose and had the kayaks full and ready to go within an hour. Out at the entrance to the harbour, the water, for the first time since we had been here, looked calm and friendly.

But before we climbed aboard, Dad made a suggestion.

"Dylan, why don't you and I take one more quick look inside the mayor's house? And we'll check out that burning cigarette of yours. I'm sure it'll be easily explained when we look into it thoroughly. Then we can all leave here without any demons. That would be a start anyway."

The fact that we were about to go had raised my spirits considerably and I had no objection to a farewell investigation. Actually, I had been turning yesterday's events over in my mind and was starting to think that maybe there were answers to many of these so-called mysteries.

Up we went to the mayor's house, Mom waiting near the kayaks down below. As we neared, I looked over at the cemetery woods. Everything looked normal.

But something seemed amiss at the house. First of all, the door was open. I knew we hadn't left it like that; in fact, we had made a point of pulling it tightly shut. We both knew that winds couldn't have blown that thick wooden door open. And when we entered, there were traces of mud on the floor.

Believe it or not, that didn't surprise me. The more I reflected on the burning cigarette, the carved desk in the schoolhouse, the phantom faces in the windows, the more I was putting two and two together.

Dad had smiled at the open door, trying to look calm for me though obviously a little spooked, but when he saw the mud he grew very serious and silent. Entering the house just behind him, I was thinking about the fresh dirt on the floor in the boy's bedroom. It made sense now.

Dad walked carefully to the foot of the stairs as though treading on thin ice. I thought of the muddy boots I had seen on the wharf at Argentia, of a voice asking too many questions and another saying, *"Do not go to Ireland's Eye."*

Suddenly the front door slammed behind us.

A big man reached out and threw my father to the floor. Two others helped to pin him down, while a fourth shot forward and made a grab for me.

"Why didn't yu *leave* like yu were supposed to?" shouted one of them. I instantly recognized the voice, gruff and with a slight accent. It belonged to the old Newfoundlander, and his face was red with anger.

"Run, Dylan!" yelled Dad, as he wriggled free for an instant and tripped the man who reached for me.

Up the stairs I went at full throttle, the man in close pursuit.

"Tie him to the stove!" I heard the old Newfoundlander bellow below me. "I'll go down and get the woman. The boy goes beside his nosy father!"

But the boy wasn't having any of that. Going through the door of the kid's room I turned suddenly and slammed it in the thug's face, knocking him back into the hall and drawing a few swears out of him. I remembered an old hockey stick the kid had in the corner of the room. It was vintage 1950s, straight as a brick and twice as heavy. When the man rose and charged through the doorway I stepped back and gave him the best two-hander I'd ever dished out. It hit him right between the shoulder blades and felt like chopping wood. My coach would call that a good penalty.

As the man reeled again, I saw his face: the same friendly one that had spoken to me at Argentia. I sprang back into the hall, down the stairs right past the men tying up Dad, and straight out the front door. Then I hightailed it to the woods.

As I ran as hard as I could, never pausing to look back, my mind was racing. Soon the events of the past few days became even clearer to me. The old Newfoundlander and his pals had been trying to keep us away from Ireland's Eye from the minute they discovered we were coming here. They found out about us on the wharf and must have booted it out by motorboat and set up shop before we arrived. Then they started trying to scare us off the island. I was the kid, the one they could really terrorize, so they had worked on me.

In a way, it was a relief—I wasn't losing my mind and I hadn't been seeing things. These people sure weren't here on their summer vacation; they were up to no good and didn't want anyone anywhere near Ireland's Eye.

But now, they had my mom and dad.

I MUST HAVE RUN for half an hour, or at least it seemed that long. A few minutes into the woods the land began to slope upward and then became very steep. I felt like I was running up a mountain, but I kept going, my legs leaden. I didn't stop until I was absolutely exhausted and well down the other side of the mountainous hill. At first I heard shouts behind me but gradually the voices got fainter, and when I stopped, bending over and heaving deep breaths, I heard nothing behind me at all.

I spotted a bunch of trees that had fallen over and climbed under them. They almost formed a little tunnel, so I lay flat on my back looking up through a couple of tiny openings at the sky. My heart was pounding so hard I thought it would jump right out of my chest. When people in the movies are in a bar or a cafe or something, and expecting danger, they always keep their backs to the wall, their eyes on the entrance. That's what I had in mind.

Ten or fifteen minutes later I heard a rustling in the

leaves in the distance. Then I heard voices. Before long they seemed farther away but then one of them must have turned. I could hear him thumping along in the woods, coming straight towards me!

In minutes he was so close I could hear him breathing. He came right up to my hiding spot. I saw his muddy boots through an opening, just centimetres from my face! He stood there for about a minute, huffing and puffing. I glanced up and saw his eyes shifting around. *Please don't look down.* But then he did! In fact, he was peering straight at me! He started bending over, his face coming down like a giant's regarding a tiny object. But when he got close he just plucked something with his hand and rose again. It was a bakeapple berry, a small orange-yellow fruit that grows wild in Newfoundland. He popped it into his mouth and turned to walk away.

Then I felt a sneeze coming on. I prayed he would be well out of earshot when I had to let it loose, but he'd only gone about thirty metres when it just exploded out of me, my hands pinned to my nose to cover the noise. I could hear him stop, turn, and then come back. His boots stopped within centimetres of me again. We both listened for what seemed like an eternity. Finally he moved. Then I heard his boots in the woods, sounding fainter and fainter as he walked away.

I must have stayed there for hours after that, listening to the wind blowing through the trees, hearing the ocean in the distance. Every now and then I thought I heard more footsteps and froze.

But no one came.

It seemed to me that they had decided to wait me out. They knew I had no food, that I was easily scared, and that I'd have to spend the night in the woods. So they called off the search and began giving me the silent treatment. I guess they figured that before long I would come to them. As I lay there, eyes darting around, no sound seemed to be coming from the area near the now-distant village.

I thought about getting up and retracing my steps, sneaking out to a vantage point near the church and doing a little spying so I could figure out how in the world I might get out of this. But it seemed too risky, way too risky. And anyway, I was too frightened even to move.

But after lying there like a corpse for a few hours, I started to calm down. I had to do something, even if it was just seeing if the enemy was nearby. Cautiously, expecting an arrow to come straight at my nose or something, I poked my head out from my hiding place.

Nothing. Quietly I got to my knees, pulled myself out from the fallen trees and stood up.

There was a rustling in the woods and something was coming towards me! I turned and saw a dark shape scurry through the leaves. Now I was really done for. I looked straight at my enemy, facing the end.

It was a chipmunk. A big, bad chipmunk.

I spent much of the daylight on the far side of the island near the water, my brain barely in gear. I was full of fear and couldn't think straight. I stayed away from the other ghost town at Black Duck Cove. Even though there were hardly any buildings there, I couldn't face it now—I walked along the shore some distance away. My head shot around every time a bird flew from a tree or anything moved in the bush behind me.

For the longest time I just walked along the water's edge, skipping stones into the ocean and trying to hold back tears. I felt like I was about to just completely collapse, and I desperately wished my mom and dad were with me. For a while I even thought about giving up. But deep within me that didn't seem right. It wasn't what Teeder Kennedy would have done, down a few goals and out of breath. Finally, I decided to try to last the night in the woods and headed back into the bush to find my hiding spot again. It was the best place to sleep. Maybe in the morning I'd think of some way out of this.

Back in hiding, with the sun going down, everything was eerily silent. I even sneaked about a hundred metres up the hill towards the village but stopped when I thought I heard voices in the distance. I ran back to my tree bed, lay down, and covered the open spots with leaves.

Waves of regret began to wash over me as my shaking hands put my camouflage in place. Why hadn't I listened to Rhett and the Bomb? We could be at the movies now, or skateboarding home, happy and without much to care about. My mind drifted back to Moore Park and the things I liked to do in Toronto. But those sorts of thoughts never lasted long because every now and then I would hear a noise or something I thought was a footstep. And there were other sounds, of things moving on more than two feet and strange rustlings in the woods. What if those thugs were the least of my worries? Were there wolves or bears or something worse on Ireland's Eye? But what scared me the most, more than those sounds, was when everything went silent. It was a mind-numbing, pitch-black silence.

I started to believe that I was completely alone on this island in the Atlantic. The old Newfoundlander and his men had killed my parents and left me here to expire slowly and painfully. I stared up at the black starlit sky, mesmerized and terrified by everything, occasionally remembering that I hadn't eaten at all, though I felt too weak to get up to do anything about it. Finally I became drowsy and my eyes closed. But not for long.

I was awakened by an enormous explosion. It was still the middle of the night. A thunderstorm was rocking Ireland's Eye. When I looked up I felt like the world was coming to an end. I could see the flashes of lightning crackling above the trees and hear the thunder rolling across the ocean like the blasts of massive cannons. The whole island seemed to shake. I had never heard or seen anything like this in Toronto. Here in the woods of Ireland's Eye I was experiencing what nature was really made of. It had taken until this night, my third on the island, to feel the famous wrath of the elements, the wrath that had drowned so many good and forgotten fishermen and sailors in the oceans of this part of the world. It was as if the weather we had had since we got here was an illusion made for us folks "from away" and reality had returned with the flick of a switch.

I didn't know what to do. I couldn't get up and run, retreat to my bedroom, to the comfort of my parents, or reach out and turn everything off. It felt like being buried alive, helplessly pinned inside a coffin with nowhere to run and nowhere to hide. I couldn't shake the feeling that this earth-shattering storm was an omen of something horrible. What was going to happen to me? And what had happened to my mom and dad?

But then I remembered the way the brief storm had suddenly seized us on the ocean and what the man at the gas station had said about Newfoundland's weather: that it was always changing and that life was meant to be that way. For some reason that made me feel a little better. I clenched my fists and watched the storm. Slowly the thunder and lightning faded and a gentle rain fell through the trees and down onto my face. When it touched me it seemed to cool me. I drifted off to sleep.

IN THE MORNING I awoke hungry and alone, my clothes soaking wet and the leaves sticking to me. But the weather had turned to brilliant sunshine and my mind appeared to have cleared a little. Almost immediately I found myself talking to my grandfather. It wasn't a dream this time and I couldn't see him, but I spoke to him like I would have to any living being. He was kind and comforting, and seemed like the grandfather I had known just before he died. He didn't ask me not to forget him because he seemed to know now that I never would.

"You're in a bit of a spot here, Teeder, aren't you?" That was his pet name for me when I was feeling down, after the immortal Kennedy of course, centre and captain extraordinaire.

"Yeah."

"Let's see: you're all alone on Ireland's Eye, your mom and dad are being held by a quartet of morons bent on who knows what, and to top it all off, you're only thirteen years old."

Then we laughed. I don't know why, but we laughed. "What do you think you should do, Teeder?"

"Stay calm?"

"Right."

"Think?"

"Right. God gave you enormous power, my boy, especially if you use it to do right."

I didn't snicker inwardly at that this time like I had in the past. His advice about God and doing what was right seemed just fine on this lonely morning. In fact, it gave me energy.

It was funny—I wasn't actually seeing him any more, even in my dreams, but in a way I was seeing him better than I ever had. He was alive again.

"Stay calm, think, do what is right, that's *all you need to know.*"

Then he disappeared, or at least he stopped talking to me. I got up, aware that his spirit was with me, and went to work. I even put my hunger out of my mind. I had to concoct a plan.

The first thing that needed to be done was to scout out my situation, regardless of the danger involved. As I made my way back towards the village side of the island I started listing my advantages. I was smaller and faster than the thugs: they were all ageing overweight men. That meant I could get away from them whenever I wanted to and that they would never be able to keep up with me in the woods. Obviously, I could take some calculated risks. Secondly, *they* wanted *me*, not the other way around, so I could draw them towards me if I needed to. Thirdly, I knew that Dad had some flares and some provisions in a secret compartment in his kayak. There was no way they could know that. And finally, I knew a great deal about Ireland's Eye. Dad had made sure of that. I knew it up and down, across and back; I knew all about its rocks and its trees, the details of its ghost towns and its history. I was betting these thugs didn't. They were here to use it for their own gain, that was all. There must be something here, perhaps something in the island's past, that would help me outsmart them. I turned this over in my mind as I came to the edge of the woods.

The church was just a few hundred metres away. I crept over to it and satisfied myself that no one was inside. I entered and quietly climbed the stairs to the bell tower. I didn't look out through the main window, but remembering a crack in the wood beneath it, peered out from there.

Below me I saw the whole sweep of that beautiful harbour again. But what I saw at the landing wasn't beautiful. Mom and Dad were each tied to a post on the wharf, and a man stood beside them, gun in hand. The old Newfoundlander was pacing on the shore, from time to time looking up the hill towards the mayor's house and the woods. I glanced at the house. There, another of the henchmen was sitting on the roof, Dad's binoculars in his hands, scanning the horizon. At the edge of the woods behind the swamp I could see a fourth man looking down at the ground as if examining footprints. He was just a few metres from where I had entered the woods at full throttle.

I turned my back to the wall and sighed. What do I know about Ireland's Eye that these thugs don't?

"I KNOW YER UP THERE, YU YOUNG PUNK!"

I whirled around and looked through the crack again. It was hard to tell but from this distance he seemed to be looking right at me. Then he turned and addressed the other side of the cove.

"IF YU DON'T SHOW YERSELF NOW, IT'LL BE LIGHTS OUT FOR MA AND PA...DO YU UNDERSTAND?" His voice echoed around the harbour.

I didn't believe him. And it wasn't just that he was the sort of man who couldn't be believed. It would be lights out for my parents *and* me if he ever caught me. But his trump card was having them alive so he could draw me to him. Then he could do us all in.

I was pretty sure he didn't know exactly where I was. His voice sounded hoarse, as if he'd been calling in various directions all morning. I bet that no matter where I had been hiding he would have seemed to have been looking right at me at least once this morning.

This was a good place to think. I could keep an eye on all of them and plot what had to be done. From here I was looking down on a map of the battlefield.

First things first: I had to get down there and get the food and the flare gun out of the kayak. I started thinking, checking on my enemies' locations from time to time. In minutes I had everything worked out.

11

THE CHASE

Moments later the Newfoundlander and his henchmen saw something startling. Up on the bell tower of the church, with his fingers in his mouth whistling at the top of his lungs, was the boy for whom they were all so desperately searching. For an instant every one of them stood stock-still, staring up at the sight. Then they started to move. And they all moved at once. Up the hill came the man with the gun and behind him scrambled the old Newfoundlander, rushing past my mom and dad, whose eyes were bulging in their heads as they mumbled frenzied warnings to me through the gags on their mouths. Down from the woods came the third man, stumbling and falling and cursing as he came, making a beeline for the church. And lastly, the man at the mayor's house disappeared from the roof, his binoculars swaying around his neck, almost falling through the hole they had punched through the shingles.

"STAY THERE, YU STUNNED LUG NUT!" screamed the old Newfoundlander at the lookout man. "STAY WITH THE STASH AND KEEP YER DAMN GLASSES TRAINED ON MA AND PA! WE'LL HANDLE THIS!"

The lookout man's head reappeared in the hole on the roof and then, puffing and groaning, he lifted himself back up and fixed his binoculars on Mom and Dad. (Glancing down, I noticed Mom defiantly holding her face up towards him, as if she were trying to stick out her tongue.)

I wanted to see the whites of their eyes. I wanted them to be so close that they thought they could nab me with ease. Up they came, snarling and wheezing, glancing up at me from time to time as if to confirm what they could hardly believe. Just to really irritate them I gave a little performance.

"*Do not go to Ireland's Eye!*" I yelled like a smart aleck in a mock-scary voice that sounded as if it came from an idiot. The old Newfoundlander looked up and cursed.

When they were within fifty metres, right at a point where the hill was very steep and they would have to keep their eyes fixed on the rocks for a few minutes, I left the steeple and raced down the stairs. I knew exactly where I was going.

The day Mom and Dad and I had been in the church and I had stood in the pulpit to give my little speech, I had noticed a door just to the left of the choir loft, on the opposite side from the bell tower door. It made sense to me that it led to the minister's chambers and that he had his own exit from the building. In fact, I was counting on it. If I was wrong I was a goner. It occurred to me as I turned the corner at the bottom of the stairs and came out onto the ground floor that perhaps I should have checked the door before I so bravely made my presence known. Maybe it led to a brick wall!

I raced over to the choir loft, my heart thumping, and opened the door.

There was no brick wall, just a tiny little passageway leading downward. I stepped back from the door and turned towards the church entrance, waiting.

A few seconds later the Newfoundlander and his henchman burst into the church.

"THERE HE IS!" shouted the old man, pointing a meaty finger straight at me. At that instant the third man appeared at a window and slithered indoors. Momentarily we stood there, eyeing each other. I had them exactly where I wanted them, I hoped. I leapt through the doorway and into the passageway.

"SHOOT AT HIM!" I heard the old man scream and then there were gunshots and the far-off sound of my mother shrieking on the wharf.

It's funny how fast you will move when you're being shot at. I was the Flash, Superman, and Usain Bolt all wrapped up in one. I flew down the tiny stairway and came to a tight little hallway in the basement. Up above I could hear the men's boots thundering on the floor and then the sound of them cursing as they tried to force their big bellies through the narrow doorway.

I ran along the passageway, my shoulders almost touching the walls. Soon I came to a fork. One hallway was wide and had a sign on the wall that read "Minister's Office"; the other continued narrow and headed towards the caretaker's room. I darted down the second one, anxious to keep my large pursuers in cramped quarters. But in seconds I came to a dead end. Frantic, I searched for a way out and noticed a big wooden door to my left. If I hadn't been in such terror, I would have noticed it immediately. *Calm down, think,* I heard a voice say.

I entered the room and slammed the door behind me. It had a lock. I bolted it. But when I turned to look around, my heart sank. There was no way out!

I could hear the men shouting at the fork in the passageway. Please God, let them choose the wrong one! But in seconds I knew they hadn't: they were running along the narrow hallway towards me, their voices getting closer. They steamed up to the door.

"OPEN IT!" growled the Newfoundlander.

The door bulged back and forth as they pushed their weight against it.

"USE YER DAMN GUN!"

For an instant there was silence and then the sound of gunfire directed at the lock. As I looked towards it I noticed a little door down low on the far side of the room, half-size as if meant for children. Just as the big door came crashing in, I made for it. When the men entered the office all they saw was the little door closing behind me.

I scrambled along the tunnel. It had a slight upward slant and then turned straight upward after a few metres. I had to inch my way up from there, using my arms and legs pressed against the sides. I wondered what the heck this chute was used for. In an instant I got my answer.

"HE'S GONE UP THE FIREWOOD CHUTE!" shouted the Newfoundlander from below. "I'll stay here and you two dolts get yer butts up to the woodpile! It's on the woods side of the church! Go! Go! Go!"

I heard them scurry away. As I desperately inched up the old Newfoundlander taunted me.

"I've got yu now, yu little mole! I told yu to stay away from Ireland's Eye, messin' in people's business! Yu'll see where it gets yu!"

Stay calm!

I kept my concentration and worked my way upward. Quickly the shaft became lighter and soon I was near the top. As my head inched out of the chute above ground I turned and saw the two henchmen, barrelling around the far side of the church. Below me the Newfoundlander ran from the caretaker's room, slamming the door. I pulled myself out and ran breathlessly towards the woods. But I wasn't sure I had enough time. I heard one of the henchmen yell at the other, "WING HIM!" and then the sound of the gun.

I leapt into the bush and did a roll. When I stood up I checked myself over. No blood. No holes. I darted off towards the cemetery.

"DID YU WING HIM?" screamed the Newfoundlander, panting as he puffed up to where the others were.

"I don't know, boss," said one dolt.

"Let's find out," said the other.

It wouldn't be long before they would know they had missed, so I kept running, planting my feet firmly with each step so they would chase me towards the cemetery. Before long they were on their way. I heard them crash over the picket fence and then trip over one tombstone after another. The man with the gun was screaming about how awful it was to be running around in a graveyard.

"AW, BOSS, YU TOLD ME I DIDN'T HAVE TO COME IN HERE WITH ALL THE DEAD PEOPLE! DIS WASN'T SUPPOSED TO BE ME JOB!"

What? Wasn't supposed to be his job? What did he mean by that? Within seconds I caught a glimpse of that metallic glint again. This time I was close enough to recognize what was causing it. It was a shovel. A brand-new gleaming shovel lying on the grounds of the cemetery.

When I got to the top of the hill in the woods on the far side of the graveyard, I turned sharply left, ran a few hundred metres and then turned left again, doubling back towards the village, this time on a course that would take me out of the woods near the schoolhouse. When I arrived, I was able to sneak around the near side of it, so it was between me and the lookout man in the mayor's house up on the far hill. There was no way he could see me. Then I dropped down low and ran through the long grass that grew in a gully between the schoolhouse and the wharf. Soon I came to the end of the grass. Here the land sloped down for about two hundred metres to the water. Lying there I could see my mother and father, their heads hanging down, as if crying.

I had about a thirty-second run down to the kayaks. I wouldn't have time to untie Mom and Dad but if I went with everything I had, I could get the flare gun and the granola bars! I was hoping the lookout man didn't have a gun, and if he did I prayed he was a poor shot. Behind me the goons were still a long distance in the woods, groping around in pursuit.

I stood up and barrelled down the hill.

About halfway down I heard the lookout man shout.

"HEY!" he cried. "HEY! BOY! STOP! OR...OR I'LL SHOOT!" But no shot came. Mom and Dad looked up. Immediately they began jumping up and down, overjoyed to see me alive. But I tried not to spend any energy looking their way. *Stay calm, think!*

"BOSS! BOSS! HE'S AT THE BOATS! HE'S AT THE DAMN BOATS!" I heard the lookout man shout.

Glancing up I noticed him scrambling down through his hole in the roof, anxious to get after me.

In seconds I was at the kayaks. I darted over to the secret compartment and unzipped it.

NO FLARE GUN! NO GRANOLA BARS!

I looked up at Dad. He was screaming at me, motioning with his head. I turned around and saw the lookout man scurrying down the hill, shouting at the top of his lungs. I noticed that his hands were empty and realized that he was unarmed. In the distance I heard the sound of the other men coming out of the woods. It seemed like the one with the gun was in the lead.

"OH-ER KAY-A! OH-ER KAY-A!" Dad screamed.

"Oh-er kay-a?!" I yelled back.

"OH-ER KAY-A!" shrieked Mom.

Oh-er? I thought. Kay-a?…*Oth-er!*…*Kay-ak!*

I threw myself at Mom's kayak, dug into her compartment, and tore out the flare gun and a fistful of granola bars. Leaping to my feet, I ran past Mom and Dad and up onto the wharf. When I jumped down on the other side, my pursuers couldn't see me. Glancing over my shoulder, I could see the wharf getting smaller behind me. I knew the crooks were coming down the hill towards the kayaks, all of them at full gallop.

Dad had yelled something at me as I went past him. It sounded like: "UH-I! UH-I! RE-EH-ER! UH-I!"

Flying along the stony beach and then up the hill into the woods on the far side of the village, I knew I had left the thugs in my dust. If need be I'd take another jog through the cemetery and trip them up again. But the tough part of my plan was next. How could I use what I knew about Ireland's Eye to save us? I had to think and act fast. The granola bars would only keep me alive for so long and the flare gun was only valuable if I found a way to use it. Just firing it off would do nothing. We were out in the middle of nowhere. How could I get anyone to see it?

I kept wondering what Dad was trying to tell me.

12

A RACE AGAINST TIME

It wasn't too long before I figured it out. In fact, I knew what he was saying by the time I took cover. I was back in my hiding spot under the fallen trees in the woods a long way from the village, munching hungrily on the granola bars.

"The Eye! Remember the Eye!" That's what he was saying!

But what could he possibly mean by that? We were *on* the Eye, how could I not remember it?

Think!

Well, what was the Eye, really? Was it the island? Or was it something else?

Then, I remembered the Eye.

Before we left, as part of the history lesson the three

of us had put ourselves through, we had read about how the island got its name. There had been several villages out here at one time and the largest had the church; that village and the island were known by the same name. But the real Ireland's Eye was an extraordinary chunk of rock, sitting on a cliff on the eastern side of the island, staring out across the ocean towards the old countries. It was almost circular and at its centre was a hole. Through it, the old folks claimed, in just the right light and on the right sort of day, you could see all the way to Ireland. *It* was Ireland's Eye.

Goosebumps began to grow on my skin as I remembered something else that Dad once mentioned about the Eye. He told me, with a laugh as I recall, that there were still a great many superstitions about the Eye. He said that the people of Newfoundland respected the memory of those who had lived here and believed that the Eye itself had always been good luck to the island's inhabitants. Of course, over the years they had suffered tragedies, many at sea. He told me about one old man, for example, who sliced off part of his arm while working alone in the village sawmill and had to be hauled fifty kilometres to a hospital on the mainland, rowed by housewives because the men were away fishing. But despite such incidents, the people of Ireland's Eye had never suffered the sort of monumental losses experienced by many other towns, tragedies where men went down by the boatload to icy deaths. The Eye, everyone believed, was good luck. Old folks said that taking the people away from the island had not helped the luck of Newfoundland, but if respect for the Eye and its power was maintained, tragedies at sea might still be minimized. No Newfoundland sailor worth a bucket of cod, Dad had said, would ever sail past the Eye without turning to look upon it and to salute it.

Dad had told me that story more than once and each time he added the same interesting fact. Every even day of every month the coast guard motored past the Eye. At exactly twelve noon the skipper turned and solemnly saluted.

I WEAR A WRISTWATCH. I know that's weird. I looked at the date on it. It was an even day. I looked at the time. It was 11:46. I had exactly fourteen minutes to get to the Eye!

I picked up the flare gun and ran.

In five minutes I was at the edge of the woods. I burst out into the sunshine not far from the church and headed overland as if I had wings on my feet. There

was no use worrying about whether or not the old
Newfoundlander and his crew saw me. There wasn't
any time for that. This was our last gasp. If I didn't get
to the Eye on time we would never leave the island
alive. Surely in two days they would find me, my
ability to elude them sapped by fatigue and hunger.

I heard them shout shortly after I appeared and I
knew they were coming after me. I glanced down at
my watch as I ran. Less than ten minutes left. By my
calculations the Eye was at least that far away.

Why in the name of Teeder Kennedy hadn't we
visited the Eye yet? We'd been here for nearly forty-
eight hours before we ran into trouble and yet we
hadn't so much as glanced at it! Now I had to find it
running at warp speed with a posse of goons after me!
This was going to be a very quick visit indeed.

I knew approximately where it was—somewhere
a little farther along the coast, probably at the top of
the hill on the far side of the next natural harbour,
ocean-ward, a huge rock with an eye looking straight
eastward across the Atlantic. But will I be able to see
it when I get close, I thought? Or will I be running
around like a chicken with its head cut off, desperately
searching for it?

I actually had to run towards the water a few

hundred metres in order to get where I was going. It was only down there that I could turn and race along an old rocky pathway that led up a hill to my left, in the direction of the Eye. From the top of that big steep pinnacle I would be able to see the full sweep of the next harbour.

For a few minutes my pursuers and I were running straight at each other. Over the dock and across the stony beach they came, snarling and shouting. In seconds I could see their faces as they flew towards me, almost licking their lips it seemed. I reached the turn about a hundred metres in front of the closest man. It was the guy with the gun. As I turned and scrambled up the rough pathway, he yelled at me. I actually jumped, shocked to hear the sound of his voice so close. Scurrying upward, I stumbled.

When I rose I fell again and for an instant it seemed like a dream, one where someone is chasing you and you can't move. The gunman was getting so close I could hear him breathing. But the next time I rose I dug my foot in hard, gained a good grip, and shot up the hill.

At the top, I turned and glanced behind me. The first goon was still close, though the others, too fat to keep up, were fading. Without pausing to look where

I was going, I started running again. All my searching would have to be done on the fly. I looked around at my surroundings bouncing up and down in my view, the sounds of the ocean muffled by my heavy breathing. What I saw was stunningly beautiful.

It seemed I could see the whole island, quiet and majestic, no longer touched by human hands. And beyond it the ocean stretched out before me like a vast blanket of blue, dotted by other islands and the coast of Newfoundland winding around on three sides in the distance. The land seemed so silent now and the water so peaceful, as if no one and nothing lived there.

Straight ahead was the other arm of the harbour and then the greatest stretch of water I had ever seen. It was endless. It touched the sky. Somewhere out there in the distance, past the horizon, were the British Isles and France and Germany and Russia beyond; from there you would come to Japan and over the Pacific to Hawaii and more of the Pacific to Vancouver and then overland to Toronto and back out to Newfoundland and this little island.

But the very first country you would see, should you stand out there at the end of the harbour and look through a hole in a rock, was Ireland!

I scanned the whole length of the arm…and there it

was! A majestic dark rock, almost circular, sitting up at the very edge of the precipice, pointing out across the Atlantic. Beneath it was a spectacular shale cliff of a most unusual shape. It formed a huge letter C, with its top hanging out over the water like a man dangling off a ledge. The ocean crashed against the treacherous shore underneath.

But something wasn't right. From here, it looked like the rock had no hole in it!

How could it *not* be Ireland's Eye—it seemed to be in the right place. Maybe the eye was very small. Whatever the case, I had no choice: Eye or not, I was headed for it. I'd have to deal with the consequences when I got there.

I peeked at my watch. There were five minutes left.

My path from here to that rock was down a slight decline through a long stretch of woods and then back up an incline on the other side where I'd have to take a sharp turn to the right and then motor along the top of the arm, moving slightly upward as I went towards the precipice. It looked to me like a ten-minute sprint, and nearly half of it was through the woods. I put my head down and ran like I had never run before.

I entered the woods without changing gears. How do you move most efficiently in here, I thought. *Think*, I heard my grandfather say. Well, what makes sense? You have to see where you are going, first of all, but you can't look down. I crouched a bit as I ran, and I tried to use my peripheral vision. That's something coaches always talk about in hockey, being able to see things without looking directly at them. I remembered reading a book once about high-wire walkers and learning that they never looked directly at the wire. Their eyes were cast slightly ahead of them, though they saw the whole wire, from the point where their feet touched it out to great distances in front of them. I looked in front of me, but tried to be aware, peripherally, of the stumps and logs beneath me. Much to my surprise I flew.

Before long I was bursting out of the far side of the woods and making the turn along the grassy land at the beginning of the arm. I glanced down at my watch again. Two minutes to go. I could see the rock now, but it looked five minutes away. I remembered seeing a clip of an old commentator named Howie Meeker talking about "afterburners" on *Hockey Night in Canada*, explaining how a speedy player gets going at what looks like top speed and then turns on the afterburners and goes even faster. If I had any such things, I had to use them now. Howie Meeker, rookie of the year in 1946, right wing with the immortal Teeder, on the ice when

Barilko scored. I turned on the afterburners.

But what I heard next almost stopped me in my tracks: the crunching sound of the hurried footsteps of the man with the gun. He was already out of the woods and lumbering towards me. It hardly seemed possible, but he was gaining ground. We tore along the grass and then onto the rocks. I couldn't help glancing back at him every ten strides or so. He was less than fifty metres away!

A minute to go.

There was the rock right in front of me. I could hit it with a slapshot from here.

"I'S GOT YU NOW, YU LITTLE MOLE!" screamed the gunman in an ugly voice. He was about twenty strides behind me.

Thirty seconds.

He was ten steps behind.

Twenty seconds.

He started reaching out with his hands.

Ten seconds.

I came to the rock. It was three metres high. But there! *There* about halfway up was a little hole about the size of an eyeball! A few feet below it a piece of the rock jutted out. I leapt at it, planted one foot on it, lifted the other one, and jammed it straight into the eye of

Ireland's Eye.

Just as my first foot left the rock the gunman threw down his gun and reached for me. He just missed. Now I was struggling, reaching for the top of the rock, trying desperately to pull myself up. He jumped and caught my foot! *Help me, Grandpa! Help me!*

My running shoe came off in his hand. I heard him curse and throw it. It went sailing, in a long looping arch, out over the precipice and down into the ocean below.

He swung at my foot again. But I pulled it up and with one great heave landed myself on the top of Ireland's Eye. For an instant I turned and looked down at my enemy. There was hate in his eyes—he was, in my grandfather's words, spitting mad. I smiled at him.

Now he was climbing the rock, coming towards me at twice the speed I had risen. I pulled the flare gun out of my pocket and glanced out to the ocean.

No coast guard!

But then I scanned towards the opening of the village harbour and saw it, puttering along without a care in the world. I prayed on the grave of Bill Barilko that I wasn't too late. There would only be an instant, right at noon, when the captain would look the Eye in the eye and give it a salute.

Hoping it wasn't too late, I took the flare and put it to

the barrel of the gun. At that moment the man grabbed my foot and yanked. The flare dropped from my hands, hit the rock and, in an agonizingly slow descent, fell over the edge and dropped down the far side of the precipice, following my running shoe into the ocean.

"DAMN!" I cried.

The man pulled himself up onto the rock and struggled to his knees. I snatched the other flare out of my pocket—the last one. I snapped it into the gun. The man rose.

We looked at each other.

"Don't do it!" he said.

But I fired. Up went the flare—that beautiful, smoking, bursting red flare shot into the blue sky of Ireland's Eye. For an instant we both turned and watched it. And then we looked at the coast guard. We stood there for a long time, both of us silent. He hoping the captain's watch was fast and me hoping it was just a little slow.

For a second it seemed as if the coast guard boat actually came to a full stop. And then it turned. It was making a bee-line for Ireland's Eye cove, and Mom and Dad!

"YES!" I shouted. "YES!"

"Yu little rat! Yu—" screamed the man.

But a snarling voice from below cut him off. "Get down from there, yu bozo!" shouted the old Newfoundlander, standing there red-faced and frantic. "We've gotta get out of here, *fast!* We've gotta make it back to the boats before that damn coast guard does! Forget about the boy!"

They had been standing less than fifty metres away, huffing and puffing, watching the flare arc into the sky, waiting to see if the captain had seen it. Now they turned tail and ran.

The gunman scowled at me and descended the Eye. I looked back towards the boat and watched with satisfaction as it steamed through the opening into the harbour.

That was a mistake. Lesson One when dealing with scum: never turn your back on them.

As the goon was descending the Eye he had noticed that I was looking the other way.

"Take the money out of my pocket, will yu, yu little rat!" he said under his breath. Then he shoved me.

I fell from the Eye and hit the ground with terrific force. I had been pushed so hard that I kept spinning when I landed. In a flash I was rolling over the edge of the precipice!

As I fell, I had the strangest thought. It wasn't a deep

feeling about my short time on earth, or an image of my grandfather. My life didn't pass in front of my eyes. It wasn't a profound thought. It just seemed funny to me that after saving Mom and Dad, it would be me who would die, and I would do it by falling from Ireland's Eye.

13

THE BOY

It's amazing how many notions can run through your mind in a split second of extreme danger. First came the almost comical realization that I was about to die after saving my parents. Then I heard *this is why I came to Ireland's Eye* running through my mind. I had been trying to figure out what had drawn me here ever since last summer. It had seemed to me that it was something mystical. When the storm was about to drown me at the entrance to the island, I thought for a moment that I understood what it was all about. Now I knew for sure. I had come here to die.

But there was more than that running through my tiny mind, thank goodness. What came to me next was much more reasonable. *Save yourself,* a voice said. It wasn't my grandfather or my mother or father or some mysterious presence on Ireland's Eye. It was my own voice, plain and direct. So I did.

Shooting both arms out towards the rock, I grabbed for something, anything. My fingers raked along the hard surface like fingernails on a blackboard. But the rocks were rough-edged and soon I had a grip. Now I was dangling by my fingers over the ocean.

That was when I came to value the concept of preparation. Had I not gone through all the training to get myself ready to come to Newfoundland, I would never have been able to save myself at that moment. Part of getting ready had been weight training and by early this summer I had succeeded, once, in bench-pressing my own weight. Lifting myself up onto my elbows now would mean hoisting my whole weight, and with the adrenaline flowing the way it was I'd have the extra strength necessary. Slowly but surely I pulled myself up and put one entire arm and then the other over the top. From this position I hauled the rest of my quivering frame back onto solid ground.

I lay there for a full five minutes, my heart pounding, staring straight up into the sky. Before long an eagle floated by, just a speck in the distance. I'd better get up, I thought, before he figures I'm dinner.

When I got to my feet my legs were still shaking. There was no need to run back to Mom and Dad. I only had one shoe now anyway, so I would hardly move at a gallop. And the henchmen were finished. They would never get there before the coast guard, and they would never try to get away without retrieving their stash. So they were in an impossible situation. If they tried to high-tail it to the woods, the coast guard would send for whatever reinforcements they needed and track them down. Their boats were tied to the dock, and in order to go anywhere they *had* to have their boats. There was no escaping Ireland's Eye. They couldn't even make a quick run for their goodies—Mom and Dad knew where they were hidden. *"Stay with the stash*!" the old Newfoundlander had yelled at his lookout man at the mayor's house just before they started chasing me, in earshot of all of us: me, Mom, and Dad. Just exactly what that stash was I didn't know, but I *did* know this: those thugs were caught in a trap of their own making and it seemed like a perfect place for people like them.

Passing by the Eye, I ran my fingers along it, set my hand on the ridge I had dug into with my foot and thought about how terrified I had been just a few minutes ago. But that moment now seemed like a dream or a movie of some sort; no one else will ever quite understand what it felt like. It must have been that way for Bill Barilko too.

Three or four hobbling steps on my way back to the main harbour, I remembered that I hadn't even bothered to look through the eye of the Eye. I walked back to it, stood on my tiptoes, pressed my eye right into the hole and gazed out. It was remarkable. My eye fit into it as though it had been moulded for me. But I didn't see Ireland. All I saw was the horizon. Beautiful beyond belief, but in the end, just the horizon. There was no magic in Ireland's Eye, I thought, and I had not been sent here for any reason. It was just a trip, a good one, mind you, and full of an adventure I would never forget, but really just a trip.

Getting down from the Eye again, I turned and headed back towards the harbour. I hadn't walked for more than a minute when I saw something white lying on the ground. At first I thought it was a book, but it was really only part of one, a chapter that someone had torn out. "A Brief History of Ireland's Eye" read the first page. As I flipped through it, it seemed that every sheet was clean and white, as if they hadn't been read. Then I found one that was soiled and marked with a pen. The instant I began reading it I knew it had fallen from the clothing of one of the thugs. I also knew something else.

IT SEEMED TO TAKE me an hour to get back. And it wasn't just because I took off my remaining shoe and walked in bare feet. No, I just took my time and stared out at the ocean and the islands nearby. I paused in the woods to look at the trees I had rushed past so quickly just a short time before. What am I becoming, I thought, laughing to myself, some sort of a nature lover like Mom and Dad?

Later, as I looked down from the top of the hill, I could see the coast guard boat at the wharf. Mom, Dad, and the captain were talking to the handcuffed crooks, frantically motioning up the hill in the direction I had fled. One thug made a shoving motion in the air as he talked and then a slight falling action, like someone toppling off a pedestal. As Mom listened to this she collapsed to her knees and Dad started running, tearing up the path towards the Eye.

A strange thought passed through my mind. As far as anyone knew, I was dead. Right now, this very instant, I was dead. So what if I stayed here? I could easily hide from Dad, and watch him search for me from a good vantage point. He would look all around the Eye and then peer over the cliff and perhaps see my shoe floating in the ocean. Imagine something else: what if

I could get off the island on my own somehow and get back home? I remembered a part of *The Adventures of Tom Sawyer* where Tom and Huck were lost on an island and then came back to see their own funeral. That's got to be every kid's dream. Imagine seeing all those people sobbing over you; imagine the looks on Rhett and the Bomb when I suddenly appeared, back from the dead!

But going to your own funeral was for storybooks.

"Dad! Dad! Up here!"

I wanted to live, and when I *did* die, I wanted people to remember me for what I had accomplished, not for what I might have been.

And when I saw my dad throw up his hands and actually give a shriek of joy to see me alive, I knew it wasn't in me to put them through that sort of pain. It would even be okay if he said he loved me.

He was still shouting now as he ran towards me. Down below, Mom, good old guilt-ridden, smart aleck Mom, who I would never trade for another mom, rose to her feet and cried out as she spotted me doing a barefoot sprint down the hill towards Dad.

I leapt into his arms and he told me he loved me. I didn't bother to scoff, not even inside.

"They told us they killed you!"

"They lied."

"You remembered the Eye and the story about the coast guard. I knew you would!"

"From now on, Dad, when you're telling a story, I'm all ears."

MOMENTS LATER, AFTER BEING reunited with Mom, I watched the coast guard load the men onto the boat. The captain was very apologetic, as if he felt the need to take some personal responsibility for the actions of a few bad Newfoundlanders. Dad told him it was not only the most beautiful province he had ever been in but the friendliest, and if the captain wanted to see, as Dad put it, "some truly badass dudes," he should pay a quick visit to our "neck of the woods."

But I wasn't paying much attention to their conversation. I was waiting for a chance to speak to the old Newfoundlander. There were things I had to ask him. When he was about to make his way on board, I asked the captain if I could speak to him. He was immediately collared and shoved in front of me.

"How did you do some of those things?"

"Yu means the ghosts?" he snarled.

"Yes."

"Well, it wasn't very complicated. We had yu goin' right from the start, that was the main ting. If yu get people into the right frame of mind they'll believe anyting, eh? I heard yu barkin' about comin' here and we couldn't have that. We've been usin' this here place to stash loot for over a year now. No one comes here no more."

"No one? I thought people visited it as a sort of tourist attraction."

"Not in kayaks. Folks get brought out here in motorboats from time to time, sure. But buddy here knows all the guys who run those outfits and their schedules too, so we can keep tabs on them easily. But in those dinghies of yers? That's somethin' else. In all my born days, I've never seen that before. We didn't know how long yu'd take, when yu'd get here, how long yu'd stay. And we couldn't even hear yu comin'. We had to set it up so yu'd get the hell out almost the minute after yu got here. So we rigged a few tings, some ghosts." He laughed.

His laughter seemed a bit uncalled for.

"The cigarette?"

"Didn't yu see that there spyglass?"

"You did that?"

"Sure. Worked didn't it?"

"And my name carved in the desk?"

"Did that the night before. And then I snapped that there map up and down a few times, and then we popped our heads in and out of a few windies when yu were snoopin' around with those binocs of yurs. We even lay in the grass by the boats to see if yu might tink yu saw a ghost. Did yu?"

"Yes."

"Rang the bell in the church."

"Right."

"Tipped over some gravestones. Damn lucky ting yu tripped over one that seemed to spook yu."

"Well, the boy on the headstone was almost exactly my age."

"Really? That was a bit o' luck. Too bad it didn't work better."

He turned away from me and walked on board, his hands in cuffs, stepping carefully as the boat rocked. I turned away myself. Not far from us the captain was coming briskly out of the boat and approaching Mom and Dad.

"That was St. John's on the radio," he said. "These characters have a list of bank jobs and drug charges as long as a minke whale. Seems like they thought Ireland's Eye was a good place to stash stolen money."

"That's not the only reason they're here," I said.

"What?" asked the captain, looking at me with surprise.

"What do you mean, Dylan?" asked Mom. It was the voice she used to talk to adults.

I reached into my back pocket and pulled out what I'd found near the Eye. They all leaned forward, anxious to see what it was. I glanced at the old Newfoundlander. He had noticed what was in my hand and his head had dropped.

"This is from a book about Newfoundland history," I said, "and this section is about Ireland's Eye. Do you see this page? It's about the cemetery. It reads, 'The people of Ireland's Eye had a practice of burying their most valued possessions with them.'"

"So?" said the captain.

"There's a shovel—a brand-new shovel—up in the cemetery."

My parents and the captain looked like they'd seen a ghost. Then the colour in the captain's face turned distinctly redder. He snapped his head around towards the old Newfoundlander and snarled. "Grave robbin' eh, me darlin'? Isn't that a fine practice for a gentleman like you?"

"But they mustn't have even read the whole paragraph," I said, cutting him off. "Because it says just a few sentences later that in Ireland's Eye your most valued possession was your soul. Jewels and that sort of thing were always passed down to the next generation."

With that the captain started laughing. Then he turned towards the men in handcuffs and really let out a roar.

But I was walking back towards the old Newfoundlander. I had forgotten to ask him one last thing, the most important thing.

"Dylan?" asked Mom, but I paid no attention.

When I got close to the old man he wouldn't look at me. He just started talking quietly. "We wouldna disturbed any corpses, my son. We just woulda looked around the coffins and set 'em back, nice and peaceful-like. These people here they lived hard lives, I know, believe me, I was born in a place like this. The same ting happened to me mudder and fadder as happened to them. We wouldna disturbed any corpses. We were only trying to scare you too."

"I have another question."

"I'll tell yu anyting I know."

"What about the boy?"

He looked up at me, a genuinely puzzled expression on his face.

"What boy?" he asked.

I smiled. "You know, the boy you planted in the

woods to chase me around and act like a ghost. He was dressed in clothes from a hundred years ago, all torn up…you know."

The old Newfoundlander shook his head.

"I don't know nuttin' about no boy," he said.

A chill ran down my spine.

"You know," I repeated, laughing nervously this time, "the boy…in the woods. What, did you have a little person here with you or something?"

He looked at me for a long time.

"There ain't been no boy around here—no boy udder than you—in generations, my son." His voice was deadly serious. "Anybody who's ever been here who was a boy ain't no boy no more. They're all gone. Everyone and everyting is gone from here, yu understand? Everyting. Yu didn't see no boy in the woods, not here…. Impossible."

I could hear one of the coast guard crew teasing the other gang members not far away. "I hope you didn't make a slip-up, boys," he needled, "and let any of those dead people out of their graves."

We stayed on the island that night. I insisted. At night I got up, wide awake, and walked up the path past the church and into the woods. I stood by the tombstone of William Snow and called out to him. But he never came.

WHEN I LIE IN my bed at night these days listening to the traffic outside, I often think about Ireland's Eye. It's still out there, alone in the ocean, miles and whole lifetimes away from where me and Rhett and the Bomb are killing time on skateboards in Toronto. The houses sit defiantly upright, the church holds on proudly, and the graveyard, that unforgettable graveyard, despite the trees that try to bury it, still guards the memories of people who were once so alive.

Sometimes in class when I look out the tiny windows, I don't see the McDonald's signs and the busy street below—instead it's miles of trees, rocky hills, and the sound of waves hitting the shore.

I've never been a particularly good student but I'm doing okay, almost as well as that report card showed the semester before we went on our trip. My best class is history now. I'm a whiz at it. I never forget a date, never misplace a face, and never sneer at the things that people did before my time. I figure I owe it to Grandpa, and to William Snow.

THE
END

July 2018:

THE SECRET OF THE SILVER MINES

Dylan and his parents head to Cobalt, Ontario, to retrieve a silver fortune—trouble is, the last person who saw it has been missing for years.

October 2018:

BONE BEDS OF THE BADLANDS

Dylan and his best friends, Terry, the Bomb, and Rhett, head to the Alberta badlands, where a seven-foot killer known only as "The Reptile" is on the loose.

April 2019:

MONSTER IN THE MOUNTAINS

Dylan and his parents take a leisurely trip to British Columbia's Rocky Mountains—that is, until his Uncle Walter pulls him into the heart of a hunt for the deadly Sasquatch.

July 2019:

PHANTOM OF FIRE

Entering his sixteenth year, Dylan is troubled by the recent loss of a friend and starts to feel isolated. His parents take him on a relaxing trip to New Brunswick's Bay de Chaleur—until he stumbles upon a strange girl on the beach and the ancient burning Phantom Ship of East Coast folklore.

Available for pre-order at Nimbus.ca, or your favourite bookstore.

ABOUT THE AUTHOR

Shane **Peacock** is a novelist, playwright, journalist, and television screenwriter for audiences of all ages. Among his novels are *Last Message*, a contribution to the groundbreaking *Seven Series* for young readers, and *The Dark Missions of Edgar Brim*, a trilogy for teens. His picture book, *The Artist and Me*, was shortlisted for the Marilyn Baillie Award. His bestselling series for young adults, *The Boy Sherlock Holmes,* has been published in twelve languages and has found its way onto more than sixty shortlists. It won the prestigious Violet Downey Award, two Arthur Ellis Awards for crime fiction, the Ruth & Sylvia Schwartz Award, The Libris Award, and has been a finalist for the Governor General's Award and three times nominated for the TD Canadian Children's Literature Award; as well, each novel in the series was named a Junior Library Guild of America Premier Selection. Visit shanepeacock.ca.